HEARTH, HOME, AND HAVOC

A Magical Romantic Comedy (with a body count)

RJ BLAIN

Contents

HEARTH, HOME, AND HAVOC
A MAGICAL ROMANTIC COMEDY (WITH A BODY COUNT)
BY RJ BLAIN

Warning: This novella contains excessive humor, excitement, adventure, magic, romance, and bodies. Proceed with caution.

Dakota never intended to become the single mother of a goddess. To make matters worse, her daughter hadn't quite figured out her role in the grand scheme of things.

Havoc isn't supposed to be part of Hestia's portfolio, but where the young goddess of the hearth and home goes, trouble surely follows.

When Dakota's ex-husband barrels his way back into her life, a heavy dose of havoc is just what the doctor ordered. She just never expected to find love in the midst of murder.

ONE

As always, the Monday mail brought nothing but heartache.

AS ALWAYS, the Monday mail brought nothing but heartache. I considered flinging the child support statement in the trash; did I really need to confirm California had garnered five hundred from my bank account to pay my multi-millionaire ex for the care of our son? Add in the three other bills, and I needed a shovel to dig my way out of my financial hellhole.

In reality, I did all right. I made enough to put aside a hundred every month for a rainy day. I'd gotten lucky. Ever since fleeing a smothering, unhappy marriage, I hadn't needed much of my safety net. I chucked the bills on my coffee table to deal with later, leaving me with the child support statement and a handwritten envelope from an anonymous sender. On my way to the kitchen, I bucked up and tore open the statement to confirm Adken had, as always, received the money for Nolan's care.

He had.

Nolan's name on the paper was as close as I got to my boy—no, young man. At fifteen, I needed to think of him as a young man preparing to venture into the world.

In one month, to the day, I would celebrate ten years of freedom from Adken. The state *and* my son had sided with my ex-husband, not that I'd ever blame Nolan for his choice. With Adken, he enjoyed a pampered life of wealth and luxury.

I missed my son, but when he turned eighteen, I'd have my chance to start over with him. The first thing I'd do was reach out to him, prepared for the worst but hoping for the best. Humming a merry tune, I dropped the paper and unopened letter on the kitchen counter so I could start my day in earnest.

The sink and its many dishes needed vanquishing, and after two days of studiously ignoring them, I needed to pay penance for my neglect. Grabbing the dish gloves, I snapped them on, held my breath, and plunged my hand into the water in search of the stopper.

Instead of the plug, I discovered something else. Groaning over the probable loss of a dish cloth, I plucked it out.

A very dead squirrel dangled from my hand.

I screamed and flung the rodent, which splatted into the wall. In defiance of gravity, it stuck to the white paint before sliding to the floor.

"Oh hell no." I shuddered, dipped my hand into the sink, and found the stopper, yanking it out. Swallowing so I wouldn't add to the carnage in my kitchen, I considered my sink.

Who needed pots, pans, and dishes anyway? Would lighter fluid and fire purify my home? I doubted bleach would do. No, nothing but fire—a *lot* of fire—could conquer such a disaster.

Ditching the gloves, I hunted for my disinfectant wipes and scoured the first few layers of skin off my hands.

I hated Mondays. I was supposed to leave for work in less than an hour, and I had a dead squirrel on my floor. When all else failed, blaming Adken usually worked. Pointing at the child support statement, I declared, "This is all your fault."

"What's whose fault, Mom?" my wayward two-year-old, a newly fledged young woman and immortal goddess, asked from behind me. "Why's there a drowned rat on the floor?"

"Hestia!" I shrieked. At the rate I was screaming, the neighbors would call the cops.

My daughter snatched my child support statement and looked it over. "Is this what you do on Monday mornings since I moved out? Holy Zeus. Rats belong outside. Also, while I was practically born yesterday and may have only learned to read this morning, I'm pretty sure this says you're paying that ill-bred horse turd five hundred a month. What gives?"

Damn it. Hiding anything from a fledgling goddess took too much work. Groaning, I slumped over the kitchen counter. "I'm paying for my mistakes one month at a time."

Then, I straightened and faced my daughter. She held the child support statement in one hand and the dead squirrel in the other. I hadn't even noticed her pick the damned thing up. Closing my eyes, I sighed and counted to ten. When that didn't help, I counted to ten again.

Damn it, damn it, damn it.

"It's not fair, Mom. The sperm donor's rich, and you're—" Hestia clacked her teeth together.

I opened my eyes, focusing my attention on the statement in her hand. "I'm not. I know. Also, what have I told you about calling my ex-husband a sperm donor?"

"To not do it."

"Yet here we are. I'm going to count to thirty, Hestia. When I'm done counting, my child support statement will be on the counter, the rest of my mail will remain untouched, and you'll get rid of that dead animal and wash your hands like a civilized being. When you return, you won't materialize behind me because you think it's funny to scare a few years off my life. Am I understood?"

"Yes, Mom."

I waited.

"Hey, Mom?"

"Yes?"

"Why is there a drowned rat in your kitchen?"

Kids. "I don't know, baby. I found it in the sink. I guess the sides were too slick for it to climb out. I don't even know how it got into the apartment. And it's not a rat, it's a squirrel."

"Oh. Okay."

I pinched the bridge of my nose, closed my eyes, and began counting. A pop announced my daughter's departure. Cracking open an eye, I checked to see if she'd done as told. The statement was on the counter, the squirrel was gone, and she'd left a new bottle of dish soap and a note, which informed me a thorough scrubbing would sanitize my dishes.

Why couldn't my ex-husband drown himself in my sink? A drowned ex would make for a memorable and pleasant Monday. In fact, I'd help him drown in my sink.

My daughter reappeared in a flash of golden light. "So, Mom. Question."

"Yes?"

"What are you looking for in a man?"

Lovely. My daughter was already growing into her profile, although I suspected the Greeks and Romans had made a few important omissions in their naming of her. Of all the women in the world, how had I ended up with the goddess of hearth, home, and havoc as my daughter? "I'm not, Hestia. There aren't any good men left in the world. The smart women have already claimed them. Do yourself a favor. Don't make any deals with the devil, and should a man want you to sign any papers before marrying you, run, do not walk. He'll never love you, and as soon as you give him what he wants, that's when the trouble starts."

"I see I have my work cut out for me. Thanks, Mom. Have a good day at work." My daughter kissed my cheek before popping out of existence.

When my daughter schemed, I had reason to worry. I just hoped she wouldn't cause too much mayhem before I managed to rein her in.

PER MY EMPLOYMENT terms with my old, cranky mechanic boss, I never showed up to work before noon. Nine to noon were his power hours, and he needed to spew his profanities without a lady hearing him. The arrangement amused me; he paid me more to work less so he wouldn't damage my delicate sensibilities.

At two after twelve, Mr. Rogers belted out a concerto of his favorite swears, and I giggled while creeping through the entry to reach my desk. I put my money on the customized BMW as the source of his frustrations. The owner couldn't get her to start, and I expected to spend most of the afternoon expanding my vocabulary. So far, scobberlotcher was my favorite, although abydocomist came in a close second. I had no idea what either word meant, but my boss flung them with vehement vigor.

"Fopdoodle!"

"He's got to be making these up," I muttered, shaking my head while I worked at sorting through the stack of letters, invoices, and bills littering my inbox. When he finally stopped cursing, I'd help him in the garage, passing him tools while he muttered the sort of words young children used to cover their slips.

Inevitably, I'd leave work craving fudge.

An engine backfiring in the garage startled a yelp out of me. I twisted around, straining to peek through the frosted, oil-greased window. Tomorrow, I'd finally get around to cleaning the damned thing.

"Dakota!" my boss wailed.

Uh oh. I lurched to my feet, threw open the door, and entered hell. A mess of tools littered the floor, taking over the three-car garage like a demented, metallic patchwork rug trying to hide the concrete. Narrowing my eyes, I planted my hands on my hips. "I left you alone for one whole day, Mr. Rogers. Why has a tool tornado swept through here? And don't you blame it on the tremor, sir."

"I fixed the BMW." For an eighty-year-old man, my boss put me to shame with how gracefully he hopped to his feet. "The owner is coming in twenty. Can you hose it off so it doesn't look like I tortured it in a grease vat?"

"Please tell me you protected the interior."

"Only a smudge or two on the wheel. Won't take you but a minute to clean. I'll be inside cleaning the grime off. Owner likes shaking hands."

I rolled my eyes but went off to find the hose, a bucket, and the cleaners. With a little luck, the BMW wouldn't need more than a quick swipe with the sponge and a rinse. Armed with everything I'd need, I marched through the back door.

The once silver BMW was covered in

black handprints. "Mr. Rogers! You're supposed to fix them, not fondle them!"

He cackled. "But I couldn't help it. She's a beauty."

"She looks like a filthy harlot." Since the power washer would strip the paint, I filled the bucket with sudsy water and flung it over the BMW, attacking the vehicle with the sponge so she'd be presentable. By the time I made a full round of the car, my soaked clothes clung to me, and I bore a depressing resemblance to the drowned squirrel.

At least my boss hadn't lied about the interior; two swipes with a soapy cloth and a paper towel restored the steering wheel to rights.

"If you're trying to win a wet t-shirt contest, you're going to have to do better than that, Dakota. Long time no see," the sickeningly smug voice of Adken's best friend murmured.

I considered killing the next person to sneak up behind me. If I murdered Maxwell Timmins, could I claim temporary insanity?

He chuckled, and I tensed, clenching my teeth. "Those jeans look fantastic on you. Since when do you work on cars?"

"Since I ditched the ass and got a life. If this is yours, it's ready. The keys are with Mr. Rogers. Good afternoon, Mr. Timmins." If I shimmied around the BMW, escape wasn't far; five feet and a quick turn to the right would land me in the office, where I'd hide behind my boss.

"Wait, Dakota. It's been years. How are you? Is everything all right? Adken's been asking about you lately. No one's seen you in at least five years, maybe ten now."

I'd tried to teach my daughter to be kind, and all I wanted to do was murder the asshole behind me. "There's a reason for that, Mr. Timmins. It's called a restraining order. Adken shouldn't have threatened me during the trial where the judge could hear. I requested the order. It was granted. If you need proof, you can look it up. It's public information."

"He doesn't even know where you live."

"He's lying to you. The child support statements have my address on them."

Maxwell didn't reply, and I took the chance to head for the safety of the garage.

"Dakota, wait," he ordered.

I ignored him and marched for the door.

"Dakota!"

Balling my hands into fists, I turned. Adken's friend hadn't changed over the years. He oozed wealth from the collar of his pristine black suit to his brocaded oxfords. "What do you want? I have work to do."

"I'll cut you a deal. I won't tell Adken I ran into you if you do me a favor."

Great. Blackmail. I expected nothing else from the scum. "What favor?"

"A friend of mine has a reservation at Calgatto's on Friday night. His date bailed. Kel's not friends with Adken, so no harm done. He's not a bad guy, but he's not your type. It's just for one night, right? Anyway, there's a reservation for two under Dundalk. Deal?"

While I didn't understand why Kel Dundalk needed a date to go to Calgatto's, I assumed it had to do with maintaining appearances. Then again, I didn't really care, either. A reservation at San Francisco's premier restaurant was worth the headache.

I'd been to Calgatto's once with Adken. He'd taken me to the place before we'd gotten married, when he'd been worming his way into my good graces. It took months to get a reservation, the food was the best in the area, and knowing Maxwell, his friend had no intention of showing up, leaving me to foot the bill for the reservation so he wouldn't get barred from making another reservation at the restaurant for six months.

I'd always thought the policy insane, but who was I to complain? I had the money for one extravagant night, something I hadn't done since the day I'd left Adken. "Fine. I'll do it, but only this once. You never saw me, you never talked to me. Got it? I don't have time for this. I have work to do."

"Got it. I'll swing by if there are any changes. Eight at Calgatto's, Friday night."

I hoped the setup would be the end of it, but I doubted it. Maxwell was worse than a leech, just like Adken. "Goodbye, Mr. Timmins. Remember, you never saw me."

Maxwell smiled, confirming my worries. The bastard would betray me somehow.

Unfortunately for him, I wasn't a stupid little girl anymore. I'd be ready for anything he threw my way.

TWO

His work giggled.

CALGATTO'S in San Francisco catered to the wealthy and talented, of which I was neither. In a way, I had Adken to thank for being able to use the valet without shaming myself. When I'd won the car in our divorce settlement, the Porsche had been on its last leg. With my boss's help, I'd restored it to its full glory. It turned heads, and when I slid out of the car wearing the sort of dress Adken would've loved, so did I.

If Maxwell's friend didn't show, which I expected, I intended to enjoy myself, squandering several hundred dollars in the process. If Kel Dundalk did show up, everything else in my evening would likely go wrong. Maxwell, Adken's partner in crime in all things, wouldn't hesitate to screw me over. He'd screw me, too, given half a chance.

I'd heard him talking to Adken about me too many times. At least I could trust Max-

well to exercise caution. Before he did anything, he'd confirm the terms of the
restraining order.

I refused to let the two worst men in my
life ruin my evening. Doing my best to ignore
those staring at me, I strode to the restaurant's foyer.

The host smiled at me. "Do you have a
reservation, ma'am?"

"Dundalk at eight for two," I replied. I
wanted to lower my eyes like Adken had
drilled into me, but I lifted my chin instead.
The old me, the one who flinched at Adken's
disapproval, had lived in fear.

No more.

I still feared, but it wouldn't control me,
not anymore.

He checked his reservation list, nodded,
and picked up a pair of menus encased in
black leather. "This way, ma'am. Your table is
ready, but the other member of your party
hasn't arrived yet."

"His work has been busy lately," I said, not
certain if I lied. "If he's not here soon, I'll
enjoy my evening regardless."

That part wasn't a lie; I'd make certain to
enjoy a quiet, pleasant meal. Armed with a
book in my purse and plenty of time, I had
every intention of snubbing Maxwell if he
tried to pull anything during the so-called
date.

I'd been stood up enough times by Adken to understand how the game was played. Maybe I wasn't the perfect broodmare—I lacked the pedigree Adken truly desired—but I didn't care.

Fake date or not, I'd like eating at the sort of restaurant I otherwise wouldn't have gone to. No, I wouldn't like it, I'd love it. I'd love it so much I wouldn't be able to hide how much I'd enjoyed spending my money on myself for a change.

At a quarter after eight, the waiter came, and I cheerfully informed him my date probably wouldn't make it because of work. The second place setting disappeared, and I took over the entire table, ordered two appetizers, neither of which were the socially acceptable salad, and planned on eating so much I'd have to suck in my gut to fit in my car.

My wallet wouldn't thank me, but my stomach would.

Sometime after rescuing delicious snails from their shells and ravaging the best steak I'd eaten in my life, the waiter brought me a tall cocktail, and I recognized the classic red and orange of a Sex on the Beach. "A gentleman from another table wishes for you to enjoy this, ma'am, with his compliments. He also wishes for you to know he finds it refreshing you're an independent woman who doesn't need anyone to show you a good time."

I accepted the drink with a smile. "Please thank him for me." Drink in hand, I returned to my book. I wouldn't have more than a few sips; those days were behind me, although I didn't regret the night I'd gotten wasted in a bar and landed myself in hot water while black-out drunk. Hestia was a pain in my ass, but she was mine, and my only regret was knowing nothing of her father.

Then again, I was glad I didn't. One child support statement a month was one too many, and I didn't need—or want—some stranger's money. I shook my head, laughed at my folly, and paid closer attention to my reading.

Book boyfriends were the best. They never stood me up, never talked back, and best of all, they never betrayed me.

ANOTHER HANDWRITTEN ENVELOPE waited for me at home along with a half-assed apology from Kelvin Dundalk on my answering machine, proving the lies spewed by Maxwell, Adken, or both of them, as they'd claimed they hadn't known how to find me. My 'date' claimed he'd gotten busy with work.

His work giggled, and several thumps preceded the call disconnecting.

I laughed, shook my head, and was properly grateful I'd dodged a hell date. While dinner itself had cost me an arm and a leg, as had the dress, I refused to regret it.

I wouldn't regret it. I wouldn't regret it. I wouldn't regret it.

One day, I'd figure out why it was so difficult to be kind to myself. Sighing, I picked up the handwritten envelopes and took them to my couch, flopping onto it to discover what other bad news waited for me.

The first two words stole my breath: *Dear Mother.*

Hestia refused to write me letters; she wanted to spend her free time visiting me. The idea of writing words rather than speaking them went against everything she was. It wasn't her fault she wasn't human. Someday soon, she'd cast off the shell of her birth and become a goddess in all ways, concerned only with her divine duties.

As always, I hoped that day would come long after my death, but I understood the hard truth. Divines rarely stuck around long. The CDC claimed the average, from the limited sample pool they had, was five years. Two of them were already gone, and she'd already begun the process of untangling herself from my life.

I'd already lost one child, and soon enough, I'd lose my daughter. I'd barely begun accepting the void I'd created abandoning Nolan with his father. Adken had wanted nothing more than a son, and I'd been discarded once I'd given him what he'd wanted.

I shook my head, blinked away the tears threatening to fall, and re-read the first two words.

Dear Mother.

The letter was only several lines long, written in uncertain, ill-practiced script. My son introduced himself, apologizing that it had taken him so long to learn my address. Then, with his handwriting even shakier, he apologized for his father, understanding why I'd gone away.

The next words shattered me, and even as the pieces fell to the floor, Nolan glued them all back together again.

My son believed I'd made the right choice.

Against his father's wishes, he meant to become a lawyer so he could help families like his—like ours—fight unfair laws and put an end to the sort of rulings keeping him from meeting me, his mother.

Instead of a signature, he left a promise to write again, a promise he'd already kept.

My son remembered me, and despite knowing I couldn't reply, he'd found the one loophole he alone could use. I couldn't see him, touch him, or hear his voice, but his hesitant words on a single sheet of paper made him real.

Torn between opening his second letter so I could devour his words or saving them to savor, I made the difficult choice to set it aside. After a Saturday shift at the garage, I'd want—no, need—a little joy to get through a dull, empty Sunday. Yes, I'd save his words for Sunday morning.

Hestia stayed away on Sundays. Her portfolio demanded too much of her on the days most families spent together. Sometimes, I wondered why Hestia had chosen me. I believed life truly had an awful sense of humor. How could a goddess born to preserve the home and protect prosperity come from such a shattered family? I was grateful for my daughter's quick maturity. She saw so little of my struggles and heartache, and what she'd seen was too much.

How would she react if she learned her half-brother had written me a letter? I expected chaos and havoc. On a bad day, she might even resort to kidnapping under the flimsy guise of a rescue mission. No, under no circumstances could I allow my daughter to discover Nolan's letters.

Fortunately, my daughter was still young in so many ways, so I hid the precious envelopes beneath my lingerie, the one place Hestia wouldn't go.

I REGRETTED my decision to wait until Sunday to open Nolan's letter the instant I got to work. Maxwell Timmins waited in the parking lot leaning against his BMW. His eyes widened at the sight of my car.

"That's yours?" he blurted.

"It's not for sale. Yes, it's all original parts with machining repairs to the frame and non-engine pieces, and no, the paint isn't original. This model didn't come in baby blue." My waspish, default answer bought me enough time to lock my Porsche. "It also has a modern alarm system and a few creature comforts, including a navigation panel. That tends to make the enthusiasts cry in their beers. And yes, I did most of the work by my-self. You break it, you buy it, and you're looking at a hundred thou to replace."

"Ouch. Point made. Look, I came over to apologize. Kel told me he'd skipped on the date."

Of course. I barely restrained the urge to roll my eyes. "He was too busy banging some broad. If you must know, I had a fantastic time. Calgatto's was worth every penny, and a nice gentleman bought me a drink with no strings attached, sent with his compliments. A pity he remained anonymous; nice gentleman are hard to find. I assure you, that's a rare occurrence among the rich and famous."

"You've changed."

I deliberately misinterpreted him, staring down at my worn jeans and grease-stained t-shirt. "You're right. I'll be crawling under cars in a few minutes. It wouldn't do to wreck my nice clothes. I've got to run, Mr. Timmins. Take care of that car. She's a beauty as she is, and she doesn't need any improvements, especially not from you. If you want to tune her or add enhancements she doesn't need, hire a professional."

"Ouch. I wanted to know if you'd let me make up for last night. It was pretty rotten of Kel not to show. I'll have your dinner put on my tab at the restaurant of your choice. Not a date, but I have a friend who'd appreciate some company. If he doesn't show, phone a friend. Make a night of it on my dime. Deal?"

I recognized a trap when I saw one. "What's your malfunction? I had a good time alone. I don't need you buying me dinner or providing company. I went to Calgatto's so you'd leave me alone and keep your mouth shut. I don't like you, and I certainly don't trust you. Buying me off with dinner isn't going to work. And you know what? You're right. I've changed."

"I can tell. Look, we got off on the wrong foot. I was wrong to try to hook you up with Kel. He can be an ass sometimes. I really didn't think he'd stand up a reservation at Calgatto's."

Liar. I knew it, and the shifty way he refused to meet my gaze promised he knew it, too.

Friends of Adken didn't stay friends with Adken without mastering the arts of lies and manipulation. I remembered. If I didn't give him something, he'd hound me. I sighed. "Fine. Get me a gift certificate to a buffet. Pick one, your choice, but it can't be a reservation place. I want good food. I'll probably go next weekend. Bring the card here on Tuesday."

"I can do that. I'll pick somewhere nice."

I laughed. "As nice as buffets get, right?"

Maxwell's expression turned strained. "You're really going to make me go to a buffet to get this, aren't you?"

Victory was mine, and he'd pay for annoying me with a little damage to his pride. "Yes, I am. Bring cash. Most buffets won't take credit cards for gift transactions."

"Harsh."

"You have no idea, Mr. Timmins. Have a good day. I'll be expecting my gift certificate on Tuesday."

THREE

Sometimes, I really wasn't a nice person.

IT OCCURRED to me I should've just told Maxwell no. Even if he decided to hound me, did it matter? All I had to do was file a complaint in court and amend the restraining order on grounds of personal and business ties. One small fee later, and he wouldn't be able to bother me again.

I blamed old habits and fear for my inability to find a better—for me—solution to problems involving unwanted men in my life. Still, I'd gotten through the talk with Maxwell without informing him I'd drown him and Adken given a single opportunity.

Sometimes, I really wasn't a nice person. I should've thanked the drowned squirrel for its sacrifice—and for birthing the fantasy of drowning the worst memories of my life in my sink.

A day of oil changes might cure me of my

stupidity, and I pretended nothing else mattered. I wished I could get away with taking Tuesday off, but I couldn't. All I'd do was worry my boss for no good reason.

I survived my shift and went home to discover another letter from Nolan, which joined the first two in my lingerie drawer. Tomorrow, I'd read them, when his father and his friends wouldn't sour me on the words I wanted to treasure.

MY WORRIES PLAGUED me so much I broke my promise to myself and left Nolan's letters hidden, waiting for when I could last more than a moment without obsessing over the past I couldn't leave behind. I craved the contact with my son like I needed my next breath, but the circumstances of his birth and my departure from his life locked me in a prison I couldn't escape.

Nolan wasn't his father, nor was he a reflection of his father. Nolan wasn't his father's friends, either.

Nolan was my son.

As though aware I stood on a thread ready to snap, Maxwell beat me to the garage and left the gift card on my desk. I'd never been to the Indian buffet, but it seemed like the sort of place Adken would go if he wanted to go slumming and pretend he wasn't a rich bastard.

Damn it.

I had issues, and if I didn't want to ruin my one-sided, newfound relationship with my son, I needed to stop obsessing over his father and his father's friends. I had the damned gift certificate. Accepting it would suffice.

I didn't have to use it, although my dislike of wasting money would ensure I did, and I'd do so as soon as possible so I could ditch the damned thing and be done with it. I'd go on Sunday, I'd hide among the afternoon crowds, and I wouldn't waste time. In and out would help me escape any traps Maxwell might have set for me.

My decision lifted an invisible weight from my shoulders, and I went home that evening smiling.

Hestia waited for me on my couch, her feet propped up on my coffee table. "You're late, Mom. Is that old man trying to work you to death?"

"What if I told you I have so many problems I need therapy, but I decided to master oil changes instead?"

"I'd ask how many of them are my fault."

I loved my daughter, even though she was the living incarnation of havoc. "Surprisingly few. What brings you my way, my divine little brat?"

"I'm worried about you. You weren't home on Friday night, and no one knew where you were. You've been getting strange mail, too."

"Child support statements are hardly strange."

"No, Mom. These." Hestia held up two new letters from Nolan. "There's been one almost every day. Is someone after you? Is it a secret admirer? Do you need help hiding any bodies? You're really no good with bodies. That rat had you screaming."

"Squirrel."

"Bushy tailed tree rat. If you're going to kill the sperm donor, you're definitely going to need help hiding the body. We could put concrete-filled buckets on his feet and dump him in the bay."

Great. My daughter had graduated from havoc to homicide. "Aren't you supposed to be the patroness of prosperity and happy homes?"

"He broke ours. He can go rot in Tartarus for all I care."

Oh dear. "You realize I wasn't serious when I said you're a walking catastrophe, right? I was teasing you."

Would my child stoop to murder to go along with her usual mayhem?

Probably.

Shit.

"I'm not allowed to kill him, but nothing in the rules says I can't help hide the evidence."

"I'd be the first one they'd suspect. I'd spend a long time in prison, Hestia."

"I'd break you out."

While I was sorely tempted by the prospect of drowning my ex in my sink, I needed to set a good example before my daughter went overboard. "We aren't killing Adken. Anyway, there's nothing wrong with those letters."

"Is it a stalker?"

"No."

"Come on, Mom. What are those letters about? You're hiding them in your panty drawer."

Damned nosy goddess for a daughter! "You were digging through my panties? Damn it, Hestia! Two weeks ago, you thought you'd contract cooties and die if you touched my bra," I complained. Why did divine children have to grow so fast?

I wanted my baby back. Hell, I wanted more than a week of terrible twos and threes. Maybe other parents loathed the teenager stage, but I'd blinked and missed it with Hestia, and I'd never gotten a chance to experience most of Nolan's life.

I'd missed out on so much.

"I was curious."

I sighed. "You know what those three words mean? Trouble. Did you read them?"

"No, Mom. You'd light my ass on fire if I did. I just wanted to see if you were trying to hide them from me. You were!"

"Fine. I'll tell you, but I require your sworn word you'll discuss this with no one, not a single soul, not even another divine immortal."

"Are you in trouble?"

"No, baby girl. I'm not in trouble."

"Will my silence cause you trouble?"

"Quite the opposite. It's not a harmful secret. It just can't leave this room. It's important to me."

"Okay. I swear what you tell me won't leave this room."

"Your half-brother's been writing me letters when his father's not looking."

Hestia's eyes widened. "Really? It's really my brother writing?"

Not half-brother, brother. I found her omission interesting, but it also made sense. She lived and breathed family, and she didn't do anything by half measures. I suspected that in her eyes, sharing a mother was enough.

"It's not Adken's writing, nor is it written by anyone I know. Adken's a rat, but he's not the type. If he wanted to do something to me, he'd do it himself. It's been ten years. He would've tried something by now. He hasn't. That doesn't mean he won't, but he can't afford to break the law. He'd lose too many contracts."

Adken made his money by toeing the right side of the law while growing the wealth of his colleagues.

"You really believe they're from my brother? Can I prove it? I won't say anything. I'll snoop, though. I'm good at that."

I bet she was. "I'll think about it. For now, no. Ask me again next week."

"Just be careful, Mom. I'm worried. Between those letters and Friday night, I'm wondering if you've finally lost it."

I scowled. "Lost what?"

"Your sanity."

Arching I brow, I placed my hands on my hips. "Care to rephrase that, squirt?"

"Uh, gotta go, Mom. Have a great night. I brought in your mail." Hestia vanished with a pop and a flash of golden light.

Kids. Some things never changed.

I OPENED Nolan's letters to discover an eclectic collection of scraps, note cards, and torn corners betraying how my son had been forced to be creative to send me anything at all. The envelopes and stamps must have posed a challenge for him, too. A few bucks and school books would let him hide his activities, and any mailbox would've met his needs.

What sort of life was my son living, that he couldn't do something as simple as mail a letter without so much trouble?

When Hestia learned her brother's efforts went beyond the reasonable, I feared she'd kill Adken. Divorce should've freed me, but I remained chained. I pondered if exchanging emotional captivity for a jail sentence would be worth it. Maxwell's reentry into my life revitalized the terror, the anger, and everything else I'd wanted to forget. Had he told Adken where I worked? The restoration of the old Porsche would infuriate my ex, too. Adken knew too much about me as it was; the restraining order ensured he always knew where I lived.

If Maxwell's goal had been to screw me over, he had succeeded.

Nothing was ever easy, and I stared at the scraps of my son's life, helplessness crashing down on my shoulders and bending me to the breaking point. I sifted through them, trying to find some sort of hope in the pieces.

My son liked tennis, or so I thought; two notes came from practice schedules with his name on it. He played mixed doubles, and his

partner was named Latasha. Without a doubt,
Adken hated everything about Nolan's choice
of sport. Based on her name alone, Adken
would abhor our son's partner.

Why had I fallen for Adken?

Oh, right. I'd been young, stupid, and
blinded by the idea of a rich knight on a
white horse romancing someone like me. My
parents had loved the idea—and him—more
than I had. I wondered if Adken still spoke to
them. I didn't. They were his sort of people,
and after the divorce, I'd run from their dis-
appointment almost as fast as I'd run from
Adken's chokehold on my life.

Each letter on scraps of paper I read rein-
forced my regrets. If I had stayed, would my
son be a happier man? Would I have still had
Hestia?

Could I have somehow fixed my broken
home?

My thoughts plagued me all week, and
when yet another lonely Sunday rolled
around, I cabbed to the Indian buffet, planning to do something I hadn't done in years.
I'd drink my memories away. I'd start at the
buffet, and by the time I finished hopping
from bar to bar, I wouldn't be capable of remembering my own name, so I wouldn't be
able to worry over what might've been.

The guilt of abandoning my son would

never disappear, but I could ignore it for a while.

Never had I hated a party of one at a table for two so much before, but all of the seats at the buffet's bar were taken. I ordered a whisky on the rocks to start the show with a bang and went to get enough food to mitigate the danger of alcohol poisoning.

When I returned, my party of one had a very unwelcome addition, and while the first streaks of gray touched his shit brown hair, Adken hadn't changed all that much. He held my whisky in his hand, and he dared to lift my glass in a salute.

The drowned squirrel had to have been an omen. If I ever got a hold of Adken and his asshole friends, the only question would be my sentence. Since making a scene would ruin my chances of a successful homicide, I sat. "I'm certain choosing to sit at my table violates your restraining order."

"We both know the restraining order's bullshit. It won't kill you to sit and talk. I've left you alone, just like you wanted. I deserve a chance to have a civil conversation with you. Don't get your panties in a bunch. I ordered you a new drink."

I checked the clock on the buffet's wall. "I'm giving you ten minutes. If you don't leave before then, I'm calling the police to report your violation of the restraining order." I stabbed an onion on my plate and popped it into my mouth, hoping the smell would offend him enough to drive him away. "What do you want?"

"You're holding out on your child support. Maxwell sent me photos of your luxury car. That's not—"

"Divorce settlement property doesn't factor into your monthly payments. It's not my fault you discarded a treasure rather than investing in it. The only new pieces are valued at less than ten thousand. Your loss, Mr. Calsin. If you'd been bothered to put in a little effort, you could've had the nicer car. I'd asked for the family car. You gave me the junker."

The waitress brought me a daiquiri, and a single sip confirmed it was light on the alcohol. Damn it. I shouldn't have been surprised. "A vodka, please. Straight up, and make it a triple."

The poor woman's eyes widened, and she scurried off. Taking deep breaths, I set my drink aside. "Talk with your lawyer if you think you're being short changed. I'll be happy to confirm under angel-witnessed oath you interrupted my dinner wanting more money."

Adken's brows rose. "That's my old Porsche? Who the hell did you rob to afford the mechanic?"

"*I'm* the mechanic."

"You're a mechanic?"

I shrugged. "I started as a mechanic's sec-retary, and in the slow hours, he taught me how to fix my car. *My* car. Would you please leave? I'd like to enjoy my dinner in peace."

To keep his over-sized ego from thinking I secretly wanted him to stick around, I stared out over the late lunch crowd enjoying the buffet. A flash of golden hair the match of mine drew my gaze. The hair went right along with the rest of my daughter, and I grabbed the daiquiri and drained the glass hoping my eyes were playing tricks on me.

Nope, they weren't.

My daughter was enjoying her early dinner with a man closer to my age, and to add insult to injury, I couldn't fault her choice. He was warm in all the ways Adken wasn't, his dark hair the shade of rich forest soil, his skin tanned from time spent in the sun. I couldn't tell what color his eyes were, but Hestia seemed to like what she saw in them.

She'd grown up too fast.

"I offended you," Adken stated.

"You being here offends me, Adken."

My vodka arrived, and I waited long enough for the waitress to leave before slam-ming it back. I set the glass down, pulled out the gift card, and tossed it to his side of the table. Rising, I went to the register, paid, and gave the waitress extra on her tip for putting up with my ex. When Adken tried to follow, I closed the door on him and caught the first cab I saw, ordering the driver to take me to the airport.

I needed a ticket to get the hell out of town in a hurry, even if it was only for a night or two.

FOUR

I hated being right.

TOMORROW I'D FEEL awful about not showing up for work, not returning home, and being jealous my daughter had managed to find someone to have Sunday dinner with. Who was I to judge?

I'd chosen to write men off. That wasn't her fault. She was the damned goddess personifying hearth and home. It was her nature to need family, to cultivate families, and to build bonds with others. My jealousy stemmed from what I couldn't have, and I knew it.

It wasn't her fault she'd found the sort of man I'd think about spending the night with. I worried she'd fall into the same trap I had.

Then again, I couldn't recall a single time I'd hung onto Adken's every word. He'd promised the world to me, and I'd foolishly gawked at the luxuries the rich and famous enjoyed. He hadn't delivered on any of his promises, and the instant Nolan had been born, I'd outlived my usefulness.

He'd gotten his son and no longer needed a trophy wife.

Instead of alcohol, I needed a shrink and a new life, but when I reached the airport, I bought a ticket to Las Vegas because it was cheap. I'd spend a few hours on the strip and find some dump hotel for a few days. No one would notice one more washed out single mom in the crowd.

I hated being right. No one noticed me at all. A few glanced my way when Lady Fortune smiled at me, and no one cared when she turned her back on me.

Feeding the slot machines a penny at a time, with the occasional forays to the quarter machines, kept the free alcohol flowing, and I drank until I needed my driver's license to remind me who I was, which confirmed I'd dumped Adken's name for a fake one at the cost of a thousand dollars.

For a whole week, I hid in plain sight, cycling between drunk and hungover. Even Lady Fortune pitied me, paying for my breakdown and leaving enough left over to buy new clothes so I wouldn't have to crawl home with a week's worth of drunk funk clinging to me.

It took two days of misery to sober up,

and I spent two more days engaging in a staring contest with my room's phone.

I should've called my boss. I should've told Hestia I needed to get away for a while. I should've done a lot of things. When she'd still been my little baby, I'd had a renewed purpose in life. She'd been my reason for getting up in the morning, arriving in the world just as I'd hit rock bottom.

She was living proof miracles could happen, and that even my meager magic, a minimal perception of fire and a knack for knowing when it would rain, could work wonders.

Two weeks after abandoning everything and leaving town, I worked up the courage to return home. I paid for my stay with my winnings, and I stood in line for a cab to the airport, sacrificing another twenty for the fare.

Lady Fortune turned her back on me in the worst way after I arrived at the airport; Adken noticed me at the same time recognition punched me in the gut. His smile chilled me. Nothing in the restraining order prevented him from running into me in another state.

I'd been so, so stupid.

"Excellent. You ran away to Vegas, just like I thought you would. What good luck for me." Adken closed the distance between us, and before I could flinch away, he took hold of my hand and brought it to his lips. "Tell me, Dakota. If you could go anywhere in the world, where would you go? I'll take us there."

Before I could voice my desire to see us both rot in the darkest pit of hell I could find, my skin tingled where he touched me. My tongue felt thick and unwieldy in my mouth, which opened as though to say something, but no sound emerged.

"Don't hesitate, darling. Anywhere you want. You used to tell me you wanted to see Paris all those times I had to go alone. How about the Swiss Alps? You like the snow. Ah, I know. I'll take you to Java. You wanted to see the blue volcano, didn't you?"

I wanted to turn tail and run, but my body betrayed me. Adken tugged on my hand, and my feet carried me closer.

"That's right. You've always wanted to see the world. I'll show it to you. Don't worry. No one will miss you. I sent a friend to tell that old geezer you work for a very important family matter has come up. You'll thank me later. Come with me. I have a private jet waiting for us. I'm just glad I found you. I was beginning to worry I'd missed you somehow."

My body betrayed me again, and I stepped into Adken's embrace.

He laughed. I went numb, my body a puppet in his controlling hands. The fuzziness crept up my arm, and when it reached my head, it smothered me in cottony oblivion, imprisoning me in the silent dark.

I WANTED to hug and kiss the clumsy idiot who knocked me down the steps. The tumble hurt like hell, but thanks to Adken's talent, whatever the hell it was, I remained limp. I sprawled on the landing, blinking while I struggled to piece together what had happened and why.

A pair of scuffed, black shoes stepped into view, matched with a pair of dark blue slacks. A moment later, someone touched my throat.

At the rate my heart pounded, I expected to have a heart attack. Adken's magic choked off my breath, silencing me when I needed to speak the most. I'd throw away every shred of my dignity to ensure I didn't have to go with Adken.

"Lie still, ma'am. Does anything hurt?" a man asked, his tone soft and gentle.

What didn't? I fought my tongue, which refused to obey me, although I choked out a whimper.

"Ambulance," he barked, and someone distant acknowledge his command. "Request a vampire; there's an enthrallment in place too strong for me to break without hurting her. I can't tell if there's an underlying beguilement or not. It's a sloppy job. I hate sloppy jobs. Dangerous, stupid dick!"

Someone replied, but I couldn't make sense of the words, nor would my eyes focus on anything other than the blue slacks and well-worn shoes.

Oxfords, no brocade. Professional but practical, and definitely not the sort of shoe Adken would wear. If I had to judge the man by his clothes, I'd peg him as a cop of some sort, happily married and hard working. His shoes had been places, but their owner hadn't discarded them for being scuffed.

I really needed to make an appointment for a therapist when I finally found my way home.

"Find out who he is, where he's going, and for fuck's sake, ground the outgoing planes! Don't just stand there looking pretty, Simon."

While I managed to swallow, my tongue refused to obey. The instant I could talk, I'd tell my new best friend in worn-out shoes who Adken was, right along with the number for my restraining order.

Outside of California, it wouldn't do me much good, but I'd tell him anyway.

Someone spoke again, the words jumbled, as though my brain refused to process anything other than what my friend in oxfords had to say.

"I can't tell if anything's broken. I'm fairly certain it's some form of paralysis, but her aura's a mess, so I can't make out much."

All of me was a mess. Frustration drove me into making another attempt at ratting out my ex. "Adken," I choked out.

"Hold on. She's trying to say something. Try again, ma'am."

"The bastard's name is Adken Calsin," my daughter announced, her voice trembling from fury. "That's my mother he bewitched!"

Damn it. An angry Hestia really would wreak havoc if I didn't stop her. "Hestia," I rebuked.

"Mom? Are you all right? What did he do to you? I'm sorry! It's my fault. I'm a terrible daughter."

How wonderful. I'd barely dodged being kidnapped by my ex, and my divine daughter wanted to take the blame for my midlife crisis. I coerced my tongue into co-operating enough to say, "Don't make me put you in time out. I fell down some steps—"

"Got beguiled by the evil sperm donor," she snarled.

I couldn't force myself to correct her. "What's the difference between bewitched and beguiled?"

The man with the scuffed oxfords chuckled. "You've gotten a dose of both, ma'am. Is

Adken Calsin the white male who'd been with
you?"

"Yes," I replied, wiggling my fingers and
toes to confirm they still worked. They did. "I
have a restraining order against him, issued
in Santa Clara, California."

"Confirm it," he ordered, to someone else,
as far as I could tell.

"Her name is Dakota Pamelle." Hestia gave
them my address, and to add to my discomfort, she gave them the restraining order
number. "She disappeared two weeks ago
after he showed up causing trouble."

Uh oh. Hestia must have spotted me at the
restaurant. "You should be proud of me. I
didn't break my glass over his head," I slurred.

Not good. Why was I slurring? I hadn't
had anything to drink for four whole days.

"Mom?" Worry laced my daughter's voice,
and her uncertainty reminded me she was a
child in so many ways. "What's wrong with
my mom?"

"Could be the magic or the fall. Don't
worry, your mom's going to be just fine. She's
in good hands, so let us do our job."

For perhaps the first time in her life,
Hestia did as she was told without question.

A CONCUSSION TOOK the blame for my slurring, and once the doctors confirmed I wasn't suffering from internal bleeding, the Center for Disease Control and Prevention called in a vampire to remove all traces of Adken's magic.

The ageless woman bit me near my elbow, a place that should've had few nerves, but the pain was still so intense I fainted. When I jerked awake, my tongue cooperated, and my body felt lighter. Something in my head had changed, too, although I couldn't tell what. I hadn't been unconscious long; the nurse wrapped my arm while the vampire licked my blood off her lips.

"There were several older persuasions," the vampire announced, her attention on the doctor loitering by the door. "They're gone, along with both newer enchantments. The newer ones were high-grade puppeteer talent work. The older ones were the nasty ones. One was a suppressor, and the other was designed to make Miss Pamelle easy to manipulate. The signatures matched for all of them."

Given a single chance, I really would kill Adken. "What's a suppressor?"

The vampire chuckled and displayed her fangs, which were still stained red. "You're resilient. Excellent. I was expecting at least ten more minutes before you were coherent. Have you doubted your worth? Questioned your choices? Sought approval from people you otherwise wouldn't? Suffered from depression? Felt like you might be the problem, no matter what you do? Had trouble accepting compliments?"

I flinched at her questions. "Sometimes."

"A suppressor is a form of beguilement designed to create an emotional dependency on the caster." The undead offered me a grim smile. "That you weren't licking his shoes whenever you were in the same room with him is impressive. I'll have a talk with the CDC rep here, and he'll take care of the rest. Suppressions like yours are handled with care. You're in for an interesting few weeks."

I didn't like the sound of that, but before I could ask what she meant, the vampire left. The nurse sighed. "She's not bad for a blood sucker. She bites shallow, and she doesn't take much for her fee. Still, you'll be here overnight for observation. Don't you mind her and the CDC rep. Until Dr. Kensington is satisfied with your condition, you won't be bothered. I'll leave you and the doctor to discuss it. He'll take care of you, so don't worry about a thing."

The instant the nurse left, Dr. Kensington stepped to my side, pulled up a stool, and sat. "Because of your circumstances, I'm going to bar any visitations until tomorrow. I'm going to have you undergo a complete set of tests and have ordered a full evaluation of your mental health, emotional wellbeing, and your personal and work histories. I know it's invasive, but it's important we verify how influenced you've been by the suppression and other beguilements."

"All right."

True to his word, he ran me through a long gauntlet of tests to evaluate my health and temperament. I endured, and I questioned everything, as did Dr. Kensington.

We agreed on one thing: had I been in my right mind, I never would've gone to Las Vegas, which worked in my favor. It meant I had a legal case against Adken, as the triggering violation of his restraining order occurred where the court order was valid.

Since killing him was off the table, I'd have to be satisfied with the slow, painful death of his reputation. Murder still topped my wish list, but I'd have to be satisfied with what I could get.

Midafternoon the following day, the hospital discharged me, and to my delight, the bill went straight to Adken, payable immediately. I smiled all the way through the tedium of discharge paperwork, and I was still smiling when I headed for the doors to freedom.

I faltered when I found my daughter waiting outside with her companion from the

Indian buffet. While he wasn't handsome in the traditional sense, an up-close look confirmed he checked off every last one of my boxes for a man to turn my head. Even his eyes were my dream color, a dark green streaked with blue.

To my dismay, his arms promised strength without the harder lines of a body builder, blending being fit with a softer lifestyle.

Great. I wanted to steal the man my daughter had spotted first. I kissed my Mother of the Year award goodbye.

"They kicked us out, Mom," Hestia whined.

What had my child done to get kicked out of a hospital? I sighed and made a guess. "Did you ask for an update every five minutes? They don't tend to like that."

"I figured that out when they told me to leave. But I waited ten, usually."

For Hestia, ten minutes counted as a major accomplishment. I expected she'd develop patience as she grew into her profile. Well, I hoped she would, else she was in for an eternity of frustration. If she ever had children, I bet she'd win Helicopter Parent of the Year award without having to worry about the competition. "Patience is a virtue for a reason, squirt. Trust me on this one. You're happier having avoided the testing. I'm exhausted, so my next plan is to go to the nearest hotel and sleep for a week."

My daughter's eyes widened. "You're not going home?"

"Not until I get some sleep. I'll get a rental—"

My daughter's companion cleared his throat. "Hestia told me you'd never run off without telling her first…"

I heard the question in his voice, and I sighed. "I wouldn't. Sure, I'm not a great mom, but I do try to take care of the basics. Anyway, the brat moved out a few months ago."

He grinned. "Viktor Jenkins, with a k because my mother's almost as much of an ass as my father." Pulling out his wallet, he showed me an identification card claiming he worked for the CDC. "Your daughter contacted the CDC, as she was worried about several sudden, unexplainable changes in your behavior. She wanted someone to check in with you."

"You're not her boyfriend?" I blurted.

"Mom!" my daughter squealed. "Damn it, I told you I was looking for a man for *you*. No, Mr. Jenkins is *not* my boyfriend. Have you forgotten I'm only two? Next you'll be asking me about grandkids. Spare me, please!"

Busted. To cover my mistake, I asked, "Were you following me?" To maintain the ruse I was upset with her, I crossed my arms and gave her a hefty dose of the eye.

"Maybe a little. I'm sorry!"

I turned my glare to Viktor. "And you helped her?"

"Technically, I was the one doing the following. She tagged along. It's a standard procedure for evaluating certain situations. We've learned to trust the insights of fledgling divines when it comes to their mortal parents. While your daughter's portfolio is among the more pacifistic in nature, it's unwise to stir the ire of the deity overseeing general household prosperity."

After the tests, the warnings I'd undergo potentially major alterations in my personality, and the knowledge I'd been spied on by my child, I needed a vacation. "I need sleep before I can deal with this."

"The CDC believes it'd be wise if you have an escort for the interim. I've been volunteered." Viktor offered an apologetic smile. "There's a good hotel a few miles from here, and I've already reserved a room."

My daughter clapped her hands. "On that note, I'm going home. I'll make sure Mr. Rogers knows what's going on, Mom. I've already vetted Mr. Jenkins. He doesn't snore, he's single, and his only flaw is his enjoyment of sleeping in the nude."

Before I could splutter a word, my daughter vanished.

"That blasted girl!" I pinched the bridge of my nose, closed my eyes, and wished I could disappear, too. "I'm so sorry."

"It's not easy raising a young goddess, although I find it rather disturbing I've been vetted down to how I sleep."

"I suffer from unreasonable urges to smother anyone who snores."

He laughed. "Well, that much is true. I don't snore."

He made me wonder about the rest of my daughter's claims. "And your tendency to sleep in the nude?"

Viktor's cheeks darkened in a blush. "I plead the Fifth."

Interesting.

FIVE

Yep, there wasn't anything willowy about Viktor Jenkins.

VIKTOR DROVE a car masquerading as a stunted SUV, and I arched a brow at the candy apple red paint job. "I question the sanity of the person who thought that thing was a good idea."

Could Viktor even fit inside? Either his clothes cleverly disguised a willowy man, or he'd be packed into the tiny vehicle worse than a sardine. Having gotten a glimpse of his arms, I doubted any part of him classified as willowy.

With a soft chuckle, he unlocked the vehicle and slid behind the wheel.

Yep, there wasn't anything willowy about Viktor Jenkins. He barely fit, and when his muscles flexed, they were more defined than I anticipated. At rest, he only looked soft.

It was so wrong of me to hope he slept in

the nude so I could begin a new career as a voyeur. A few looks couldn't hurt, could it? I feigned disgust at the car to cover my inappropriate admiration of its driver. "That can't be comfortable."

I slid in, and it was a tight squeeze for me, too.

"Ah, to have earned the scorn of a woman over my car."

"If you really want to torture yourself cramming behind the wheel, I can make a few recommendations. I can't give you a pass on this one, Viktor. It can't even function as a family car. Please tell me it's a rental, and then tell me the name of the company, because I need to yell at them for cruel and unusual punishment."

"Are you always so sassy?"

His question slammed the brakes on my rant, and my face flushed. I swallowed. "No, I'm not."

Viktor sighed. "Sorry. I didn't mean to upset you. The talent used on you is similar to what a vampire uses to enthrall someone. Your situation is unique, as far as I know. I've never seen it before, and neither have my contacts within the CDC. It's a bit like a magnet. When a beguilement works as intended, the victim sticks to the controller. Your situation is the exact opposite. While there was definitely a beguilement in place, it's like you reversed the beguilement's polarity. Instead of becoming a puppet eager to please, he repelled you. The magic remained intact, but he got the opposite result of what he wanted. You ran from him rather than to him."

"How is it no one noticed this until now?"

Viktor reached down and adjusted the seat, buying himself an extra inch of space, not that it helped in the tiny vehicle. "I have a few theories, but I suspect the original beguilement was layered over a long period of time and designed to be difficult to spot. The new one was a sloppy job set in a hurry, so it was really obvious to anyone with a talent capable of detecting auras, like mine. I've been assigned to your case as I have a similar talent, although my abilities require consent of all parties involved. However, once consent is given, mine are permanent and difficult to remove."

"That's a scary talent," I confessed.

"I'm a binding arbitrator. My talent is usually used for therapy and rehabilitation, although I can witness—and implement—a binding oath. I'm often the first person the CDC requests if there's a beguilement needing to be broken. They only call in vampires on the dangerous jobs, as they're the true masters of breaking such talents. I didn't want to hurt you."

"You're the man with the worn-out shoes."

He laughed. "Of all the things to notice, you noticed my shoes? Yes, those worn-out shoes were mine. I followed you in the airport while your daughter notified security and had them call for backup. She's incredible. If it wasn't for her file with the CDC, I'd never believe she's only two. She's so advanced, even compared to fledgling divines. There aren't a lot of them, but our records show the others didn't fully grow into their portfolios until their teens, although the process begins around age four or five. While they developed faster than human children, none have grown at Hestia's rate."

"Hestia is incredible," I conceded. Then, to turn the conversation away from my daughter, I added, "To be fair, I noticed your shoes first, then I noticed your pants. Everything else was a blur."

"The type of magic he used on you is illegal. While there are legal applications for beguilements, especially in medical rehabilitation, it's under very strict conditions and usually requires a court order—or an emergency. My talent typically falls under medical rehabilitation, although I am called in to help with law enforcement." Viktor started the car, and his back popped when he twisted around to check his blind spots. Muttering curses under his breath, he pulled out of the spot. "It's a rental. I drive a big manly

truck entirely inappropriate for the city because I like pissing off impatient drivers in
tiny cars. They're too frightened of my big,
manly truck to do anything about it. I also
crush cans to show off when I'm not posing
like the bodybuilder I am."

His claims were so absurd I laughed until I
cried. "You don't!"

"Busted. In reality, I have an old SUV that
gets me where I need to go, but it guzzles so
much gas I catch a bus whenever possible.
Disappointed yet? You should be."

Wiping my eyes, I shook my head. "Only
reason I have a nice car is because I hated my
ex so much I wanted revenge for screwing me
over, and drowning him in my sink isn't
legal."

"It's unfortunately not. What I'm curious
to know is if you have a talent, or if you're
just so stubborn and headstrong not even
magic can sway you."

I scowled and turned my head to stare out
the window. "If that were true, he wouldn't
have been able to control me."

Viktor remained silent for several minutes
while escaping the hospital and its maze of
parking lots. "No, I disagree. He wasn't able
to charm you into doing what he wanted. He
had to blank slate you, repressing everything
you are to get you to do what he wanted, and
that's pretty incredible. It doesn't really

matter if it's a talent or your indomitable will. It's something you should be proud of. Maybe one in a hundred can even attempt to shrug off that sort of magic. I'd put the odds at closer to one in a thousand. You've been fighting him for years."

It didn't feel like something I could be proud of, but I didn't argue with him.

As though reading my mind, Viktor sighed. "I know this is difficult for you, but hopefully this will help. Suppressors make your strengths weaker and your weaknesses stronger. They're designed to make you pliable, not change who you are. Underneath the magic, you're still you, and I can, with your consent, help you see that for yourself if you'll allow me."

Viktor gave me too much to think about, and uncertain if I even had any other options, I nodded.

Time would tell.

I WENT from wide awake to sound asleep before we reached the hotel. Playing a damsel in distress came with a few perks, which included breakfast in bed and my ideal man brushing out my hair while I tried to remember how I'd gotten into the room. I decided there were three options I liked, and one I didn't. I disliked option four, as option four involved walking to the room under my own steam.

If I was going to end up a damsel, I wanted the whole package, including being carried like a princess, although I had a rather unhealthy interest in him tossing me over his shoulder and showing off his muscles. Along with the rest of my personality, I suspected Adken had suppressed my inner slut, because I wanted to rip Viktor out of his clothes in a bad way.

The last time I'd taken the dive, I couldn't remember the man who'd given me Hestia. If I ever learned who he was, I'd have to thank him. In my next breath, I'd decline any child support, as I wasn't going to trap a man into fatherhood—fiscal or otherwise—unless he wanted to be involved with our pain-in-the-ass daughter's life.

And if he did show up and wanted in her life, well, I'd figure something out. There wasn't anything wrong with pursuing a handsome man, although I wondered if he was actually handsome, or if the beer, the vodka, and whatever the hell I'd been drinking had skewed the picture.

No matter what the case, I wasn't married, not anymore.

Viktor chuckled, which didn't help with my state of mind at all. "That's quite the expression on your face. I can't tell if you want to kill me or if I'm on the menu. If you're still hungry, I can order something."

I brushed off my inability to remember dinner or breakfast as the consequences of a severe case of exhaustion. "Theoretical question. Let's say I decided to go out and seduce someone."

Viktor's eyes widened, and he cleared his throat, probably so he wouldn't start laughing.

While I could have phrased the opening of my question better, I blamed my repressed inner slut for having the daring to ask at all. I plowed on, asking, "If Hestia's father showed up, would I have to seduce both men? Do I get to pick the man I like the most? How does this work? This single mom hasn't been on a date in years. Is there a date limit before I can invite him to come home with me? Huh. Does this mean I'm a slut?"

"You're not a slut. It's a common symptom of suppression. If you want, I can use my talent to help mitigate the symptoms. Essentially, the suppressors make a lot of alterations to the victim, including hormone levels. Everything that's been suppressed tends to surge to the surface, so if there was a component regarding sexuality, well, the victim ends up giving even a sex demon a run for his money. Lowered hormone levels can cause a lot of problems, but generally, the magic involved keeps the body functioning as necessary. It's really rare someone has been suppressed for as long as you've been, which is why I'm here. I can, with my talent, help you control the biological aspects." Viktor's expression turned pained. "The alternative is to work it out of your system naturally."

My eyes widened. "The CDC tossed you in here with me knowing I might turn into a slut?"

He slapped his forehead. "You're not a slut. No, they put me in here with you knowing you might challenge an incubus. Yes, if you ultimately need—or want—an incubus to help through the adaptation period, one is a phone call away. I made the suggestion you should have your pick of how to handle this situation, as you've been exploited enough as it is."

Handsome man, check. Handsome man giving me full control of the situation, check. Handsome man already in the same hotel room with me, check. Handsome man capable of brushing my hair out without complaint, check. Handsome man talking about sex when I wanted to rip him out of his shirt already, check.

Best of all, he somehow managed to deliver his speech with a neutral expression and tone.

"That's kinda insane," I informed him.

"It's magic. What comes around goes around, and everything he suppressed is surging to the surface. Typically, the CDC hires a demon to sort out the biological aspects. They can meddle with a human's hormone levels rather easily. In your case, I recommended you decide for yourself. If you want an incubus, I'll call for one. If you want two incubi, I'm sure an arrangement can be made. If you want an entire pack of them fulfilling your every desire, I can make an inquiry."

"And if I wanted to rip you out of your shirt? Would you be okay with that?"

Viktor's chuckle elevated him to the top of my to-do list. "I never said I was a good man." His smirk promised trouble; I'd seen his expression on the faces of men on the prowl in plenty of bars. Bars got me in trouble.

Bars had alcohol. Alcohol led to black outs. Black outs led to sex with men I couldn't remember.

I really needed to make sure Hestia never realized she was the product of an alcoholic binge and a night I wanted to remember but couldn't.

No, I wouldn't worry about Hestia for a night or two. She could take care of herself, and she'd abandoned ship the instant she'd ensured I was going home with a man she liked.

The sneaky little brat.

"Is the CDC aware of this, Mr. Jenkins?" I arched a brow at him.

"They're aware I can refuse any unwanted advances. They're also aware I possess twisted and questionable yet barely acceptable morals, which are easily bent when an attractive woman tells me she wants to rip me out of my shirt. I only engage with one woman at a time, and to answer your other question, the socially accepted practice is to remain with your current man unless a sex demon is involved."

"That seems so entirely random. Add in a sex demon, and anything goes."

"Well, once a sex demon gets involved, common sense and morality tend to fly right out the window. It's the whole 'don't throw stones in a glass house' thing. It's hard to stay on a high horse when there are plenty of sex demons willing to start a public party. Incubi and succubi aren't the only ones who can rev a human's engine, either. Never been with one?"

I shook my head. Well, I supposed it was possible I'd gotten involved with one during a black out, but I meant to stay as far from bars as possible in the future.

Alcohol did nothing but get me in trouble.

"Well, the choice is yours. However you want to handle the next few days, it's up to you to decide."

One concern rose over all the rest. "This never gets back to Hestia. Understood?"

While weak and strained, he laughed. "I'm fairly confident she understands basic biology, but I won't shatter her belief her mother is a pure maiden."

I had a hard time imagining myself as a pure anything, let alone a maiden. Two children evicted me from the pure maiden pool. "A few weeks ago, she viewed my lingerie drawer as the prime evil. Then she realized I was using it to hide things from her."

Viktor bit his lip, but a snorted laugh escaped. "She looks all grown up, but then you tell me something like that. Then I start to think she shouldn't be allowed out in public unsupervised."

"If she wasn't so damned good at teleporting, I'd chain her in my apartment for the next sixteen years."

"You could try a leash. Restraints can block inexperienced teleporters, although it won't stop a divine for long."

I laughed at the thought of leashing my daughter. "She'd kill me."

"Honestly, I'd be more concerned about your ex-husband. She'll kill him if a chance presents itself. Divine children are often protective of their mortal parents."

The possibility worried me, but I hid my discomfort with a snort. "There's a line. I'm at the front of it."

"You probably shouldn't admit that to me. I'm technically part of general law enforcement."

"Pity. So, Mr. Law Enforcement, this is entirely theoretical, of course, but if I were to kill someone, what *is* the best way to hide the body?"

"Incinerate it and feed the ashes to a phoenix. Alternatively, as I doubt incineration is an option for most, use a really deep hole—twenty feet minimum, deeper if you can manage. If you want to make sure no one finds the body, mulch him before dumping him in. A remote location prone to rockslides is useful. If the killer happens to know a trustworthy gorgon, smashed statues are hard to identify."

"Tell me more," I murmured, licking my lips.

"I can't tell if you're hitting on me or turning me into an accomplice."

"Can't it be both?"

"Considering I've already told you I'm not a good man, I suppose there's no reason it can't be both. I've never planned a murder as pillow talk before. Why not? I wasn't all that good at the law enforcement gig anyway. I just have a useful talent. This is the first time I've been invited to help with a murder."

"There was a dead squirrel in my sink, and I thought I'd liked to drown him. But if I drowned him in my sink, it'd be hard to hide the body."

"You sound so disappointed."

"I am." I scowled. "I'd say he took my son from me, but I was the trusting idiot—"

"Ensorcelled," he corrected.

I shot him a glare and grunted. "Fool. I was a fool. There's no proof there's nothing more to it that my stupidity and greed. There's no proof he had influenced me before we got married."

"The divine don't just pick anyone, Dakota. The type of woman capable of bringing a goddess into the world isn't the type to be that much of a fool. No, I think he wanted you for a purpose."

"Our son."

"Likely. Does he know about Hestia?"

I shook my head, but then I hesitated and shrugged. "I don't think so. I've tried to keep her hidden."

"He could be insane. Putting him down would be for everyone's good. We'd be doing the world a favor."

I stalked towards him, prowling around

the bed, watching him through my lashes. "Tell me more."

His smirk once again promised trouble, and I looked forward to enjoying every moment of it.

SIX

You did a pretty good imitation of a zombie.

VIKTOR TRICKED ME, and I didn't mind a bit. He distracted me so thoroughly I didn't care about anything other than him. Instead of murderous pillow talk, I slept. When I woke, I discovered I held his arm in a white-knuckled grip. He worked on his phone, and when he caught me watching him, he smirked. "Good evening, sleepy."

Yawning proved him right, and I stretched, wincing at my stiff, sore muscles. "What time is it?"

"Seven. If you'd like to go out for dinner, there's time to take a shower if you want. We won't be heading back to California today. Until you're capable of lasting a few hours without wanting to jump every attractive man you see, *and* you can stay awake for several continuous hours, we're staying here.

Standard CDC procedure, and the room bill is going to your ex-husband."

I liked the sound of that. "Room service, as expensive as we can make it?"

He chuckled. "Would be billed to him, yes."

"I like the sound of that. Did I miss anything?"

"Remember lunch?"

I shook my head.

"I'm not surprised. You did a pretty good imitation of a zombie. You slept right through when I called in a vampire to make sure there were no additional beguilements; Annie wasn't certain she'd gotten them all, and when Annie isn't sure, I worry. Fortunately, she had. You're clean."

"Oh. That's good. Was I bitten again?" I checked my arm for any new puncture marks but couldn't find any.

"No. As there was no need, I refused on your behalf. You've been traumatized enough. Now that the worst is over, you deserve to be pampered while you're recovering."

"I appreciate that." I did, too. I couldn't remember the last time anyone had actually pampered me. Until I got a few minutes to think, I refused to worry about it. I turned my attention to the bathroom door. "Is there a decent tub in this place?"

"There's a Jacuzzi."

I bolted out of bed and beelined for the door. "You're welcome to join me."

"If I do that, we'll never leave the room."

"That's what room service is for, and you already told me Adken has to pay for my indulgences. With room service, we don't have to leave." I giggled, slipped inside the marble-tiled bathroom, and examined the tub trying to learn its secrets. "How'd you score such a nice room on such short notice?"

"Thank the CDC; they keep ongoing reservations at nice hotels as part of its operations. Creature comforts go a long way towards helping victims recover. Whenever security is a concern, the CDC pulls from their reservation pool on the top floor of good hotels, as is the case with you. If that bastard tries to get to you here, he'll regret it. I'm not the only CDC agent in the building. I'm just the one who has no scruples about killing the bastard and tossing his body off the balcony."

A chill ran through me. "They haven't caught him yet?"

"No, not yet. Don't worry. He's not going to get near you, not with me around." Viktor joined me in the bathroom, leaving clothing strewn in his wake. Dressed, he checked off all my boxes. In the nude, he tempted me; I wanted to kidnap and take him home with me.

I smiled, fiddled with the faucets until the temperature was just right, and stepped into the tub, kicking at the water. Snatching the first bottle on the ledge I found, I read the label and decided shampoo would work.

He rescued the bottle and replaced it with the larger, blue one just out of my reach. "This one is for bubbles. The other one is for your hair. Also, I owe you a theoretical discussion on the methods one might use to commit the perfect murder."

"Yes, let's discuss this." I sat, scooted over, and made room for him. "If I dig a very deep hole, fill it with water, and drown him, will his body float? Do I need to hold him down while I throw rocks at him?"

He chuckled and joined me in the tub. "If we get a long enough pole, we can hold him down until we've buried him enough to make certain he stays down." Once settled beside me, he slid his arm around me and pulled me close. "You're nowhere near as shy as I thought you'd be."

"Why would you think I'm shy?"

"According to your charming two-year-old, you're terrified of men."

I splashed Viktor with sudsy water. "Do I look terrified to you? I just have a really bad history of going to bars, getting black-out drunk, and never remembering if I went home with someone that night. I can tell you, without question, I was successful at least once."

Viktor's brows rose. "You have no idea who Hestia's father is, do you?"

"Not a clue in hell, and I've no intention of looking for him. Surprising someone with fatherhood because drunk as a skunk me forgot birth control isn't how I want to start any conversation. I also don't want him getting a monthly taunt over how I accidentally ruined his life with my stupidity."

"There should be limitations to how self-sacrificing someone can be. Also, we're covered on the birth control front. I called in a favor or two from an incubus, so I'm infertile until I ask him to reverse it. The CDC is pretty careful about making certain suppressed women don't get any surprises nine months down the road."

Damn it. I'd forgotten birth control again. "See? I'm an idiot," I muttered.

He chuckled and kissed the top of my head. "You're fine. It was my job to remember the details. You're going to have to try to remember in any future adventures you may want to go on with men unless you want another unexpected little one under foot."

I sighed. "I got short changed last time. She stayed a baby for a month. While I appreciated the limited destruction during her toddler phase, it only lasted a few weeks. She stalled out at five or so for a little while, but when your five-year-old child is playing scrabble with the librarian because your vocabulary is too limited for her, it's hard. I haven't seen Nolan since he turned five."

I'd missed everything with both of my children.

"Nolan's your son?"

I nodded.

"Well, I can tell you this much: your ex-husband's actions have put you in a position to make a custody claim. All prior arrangements, with the exception of the restraining order, are to be investigated. It might take a while to have a full custody claim pushed through the courts, and current guardianship arrangements will hold until it can be processed, but you have options—options your ex will have to pay for as the aggressor."

I splashed at the water and stretched out my feet so I could turn the faucet off with my toes. "Or we could accept I'm guilty of bouts of shameful stupidity."

"We're going to have to work on that."

"We're?" While I had to squirm and stretch, I managed to reach the jets, flicking them on. "When did my problems become our problems?"

"Around the time I decided I'd fight an incubus to be the one keeping you company. I had to play dirty to win, too."

Interesting. After the jets rumbled to life, the soothing scents of lavender and lilac filled the air. With a pleased murmur, I relaxed. "Why?"

"You deserve better, and why should I trust anyone else to make certain you're treated right?"

Prince Charming didn't ride a white horse; he wore worn shoes, worked with law enforcement, and as needed, helped plan a murder. "Are you trying to seduce me, Mr. Jenkins?"

"Yes."

I loved an honest man. I knew exactly what he wanted, which fell in line with what I wanted. And if he did want something else from me, I could always decide later, after I sorted out the messy tangle my life had become. "I can work with that, but I'll warn you now: pull any of Adken's shit, and I'll be hiding two bodies."

"If you can't trust me with anything else, trust me with this. I'll do my best to treat you far better than he ever could, as I don't want to die."

I giggled. "I can work with that. Carry on with your seduction, Mr. Jenkins. I don't have all day."

Viktor laughed.

WHILE I SUSPECTED an incubus lurked nearby turning me into a Viktor-hunting fiend, my willing victim didn't seem to mind. It took two days until I could look at him without getting certain ideas, after which I slept for twelve hours straight.

Since Viktor didn't seem concerned, I went with the flow.

Two days with him gave me hope there were still a few good men left in the world, which didn't help me in the grand scheme of things. I *could* keep my hands off him, but I didn't want to.

Damn it.

Avoiding the reality of returning to California made it easier to hide in the hotel with him, but as always, my guilt surfaced and ate away at me. I needed to go home, but I didn't want to lose the sense of security I found in Viktor's company. With Adken, my worries had been constant, and a single wrong word could trigger unwanted advances and, in rare times, violence.

The first time he'd left one side of my face purpled had been the last, but I'd never forgotten the fear.

With Viktor, I wanted only him, and I wondered if he was even capable of raising his voice. Even the times I'd woken up confused and fighting mad, he'd given me space, waited for me to remember what had happened, and smiled when the horror of lashing out took hold.

When I returned home, I'd lose everything I hadn't known I'd wanted. I'd stolen a few days of peace and pleasure, and soon, I'd have to let him go and return to my life.

I supposed Adken's attempt had clarified things for me. I didn't want to go back to fixing cars. I'd done it out of spite, to prove I could be useful and do something productive with myself. I didn't know what I wanted to do.

He'd stolen that from me, too. Day by day, as the pieces he'd suppressed stirred, the little things fell into place.

I didn't really like chocolate, but I'd eaten it because it was expected of me. I didn't like most alcohols, either. I couldn't even imagine why I'd thought it worthwhile to go out to a bar in the first place.

I loved steak far more than I thought, and I'd asked for something with beef at every chance.

The one night we went out on the town, I discovered I enjoyed wearing tight leather pants and a matching coat, and that playing pretend in a city filled with magic was far more enjoyable with the right company. Instead of alcohol, I spent the night intoxicated on Viktor.

I didn't want to go home without him. I

didn't want to face everything I knew I would have to the instant I returned to California.

A call to a lawyer could begin a custody battle I couldn't realistically afford. I could submit the unfair litigation claim without help; of all the forms California had to offer, it was the easiest, three pages of information I knew by heart.

"If you keep gnawing on your lip, you're going to chew it off. What's bothering you?"

I sighed and stared at the floor. "What isn't? I'm going home to a disaster."

"How so? Your boss was notified, and the CDC filed for restitution on your behalf. The tentative claim approval is already in; at the minimum, you're owed at least half a million dollars, to be paid immediately. They'll garner your ex's bank account sometime this week. As that's the absolute minimum, you won't have to wait for the funds. I expect you'll have the money by Friday. The CDC provided a replacement for you until you're ready to return to work, and they've authorized a six-month leave. You have time. Take the six months and figure out what you want to do with the rest of your life. It'll work out. Your ex would be a fool to come near you at this point."

"And what about Nolan?"

"I don't know. I wish I had the answers for you, but I don't know the procedures in cases like this. All I know is that you do have the choice to file for custody, but I don't know anything about how it's done. For now, I expect they'll do what's least disruptive for him, but that's just a guess on my part. I wish I had a better answer for you."

I wished he had a better answer, too. All there was left to do was add some steel to my spine, head home, and deal with the aftermath.

SEVEN

I'd have to tell him he classified as therapy.

AS I PREDICTED, I parted ways with Viktor at the airport, and as I wanted him to think well of me, I bid him a cheerful farewell. No strings attached, magically induced lust wasn't love. It couldn't be, although it made for a good starting point, I supposed.

Until I learned who I really was all over again, Viktor needed to remain nothing more than a favorite memory.

I wouldn't like it, but I could live with my choice.

Hestia was waiting for me at my apartment, and she stared at me with teary eyes. "Are you all right?"

Damn it. I couldn't lie to her, not even when she looked ready to cry. "I will be. I'm sorry it took me so long to come home."

My daughter shook her head. "The CDC

explained you needed therapy, and that you needed help I can't provide."

I choked on my spit. Coughing, I beat a hasty retreat to the kitchen for a glass of water. If I ever saw Viktor again, I'd have to tell him he classified as therapy. While I was at it, I'd sign up for frequent sessions.

If my lust for the man didn't ebb soon, I'd be a mess before the end of the week.

"Therapy is probably a good idea," I conceded. "I'll look into it."

"You're really okay? You took a bad fall down those steps."

It took gargantuan effort to keep my expression neutral. "I slept it off. I'm fine now."

"Good! The CDC told me you're off work for the next six months, and the replacement they sent to help Mr. Rogers is a neat lady. She's hoping the sperm donor shows up, because if she gets her hands on him, he'll probably die a terrible death. She's a shocker, and she's eager to give him a dose of her special brand of medicine. I really do hope she kills him," my daughter snarled.

I already regretted I hadn't gotten Viktor's address or phone number. It meant I wouldn't be able to send him a proper invitation to my ex's murder. "It's all right, baby."

"Is there anything I can do? I'm sorry, Mom. I knew something was wrong, but I didn't know what. If…"

"You did nothing wrong, Hestia. But there is something you can help me with."

Her expression brightened. "What?"

I allowed myself a grim smile. "One day, you're going to help me dig a really deep hole. Then, after all this has settled, maybe a few years down the road, when Nolan's an adult, you're going to help me locate my ex-husband. Once we find him, I'll be accepting your offer to help me hide the body. *You* will not break a single one of your rules in this endeavor. Am I understood?"

For better or worse, I'd reclaim my life and get payback for being a victim for so long.

Hestia's eyes widened. "Oh."

"Just make certain you don't violate any of your rules. Helping me dig a hole so I can hide his body is enough. Understood?"

"Yes, Mom. But why a hole?"

"It won't just be any hole. It'll be a deep hole, one so deep no one will find his body for a long time. I've learned from a reliable source it should be at least twenty feet deep. If we use a long enough pole, we can make sure he stays down after I've finished drowning the bastard."

"You're really planning to kill him."

"Turnabout is fair play. He stole my life from me. I'm stealing his in retaliation. I'm

being merciful. I won't toy with him long before I finish him off."

My daughter gulped. "I've learned something very important today."

Crossing my arms, I regarded my
daughter with a raised brow. "What did you
learn today?"

"Don't screw with Mom."

The pride in her voice helped. "That's
right, baby. Don't screw with Mom. Not only
does she get mad, she gets even."

IN THE TIME I'd been in Las Vegas, my son
had written ten letters, and the last one was
dated the day of my flight from California. I
clung to his every word, important only to us,
but an important reminder my life before my
divorce hadn't been a complete waste.

My son had lost his last match, and he
blamed himself for his failure.

Adken would've blamed everyone other
than him.

Despite all odds, my son hadn't become a
clone of his father.

I submitted the initial claim challenging
Adken's custody, and the refusal came
without a hearing, a setback I'd hoped to
avoid but also expected. Appeals would win
the war, and I decided to be grateful I

wouldn't have to wait six months before receiving a response. No reason for the refusal accompanied the notice.

It didn't matter. According to the slip, I'd be eligible to file for appeal in four months.

True to Viktor's claim, I had half a million to work with and six months. After my first day back, Hestia had stayed away.

I couldn't blame her. I'd told her the truth, and it was a dark, bitter thing.

Time away would do me the most good. I lingered a week, long enough to learn my son's fate.

Adken's parents were awarded custody, and the date Nolan's letters had stopped fell in line with him moving in with them.

Hestia visited once, and she seemed distant and distracted.

I feared my tainted heart was too much for her to tolerate; she was a nurturing goddess by nature, Nolan was in a family environment, and as far as I could tell, my days as a mother were finished.

With nothing left to tie me down, it was easy to let go and move on. I packed a few bags, notified my landlord I was leaving, and made arrangements for the apartment to be emptied.

The Porsche was too distinctive, but I couldn't bring myself to abandon my hard work completely. I put it in storage, bought a junker, and headed south. With the minimum settlement, I'd be able to survive for a long time. There were places far cheaper than California.

I'd have to return to try for custody of my son again, and he'd become my goal. I didn't want his letters.

I wanted him in my life.

The truth of Adken's magic bit deep. It hadn't changed me all that much, except for one thing. His magic had corrupted me, tainted me, and taken away my desire to know my son. Without his influence, I never would've given up my son without a fight.

Death was too kind for my ex-husband, but unless I found him, I'd satisfy myself with a deep hole only I knew about, just in case a chance presented itself. I'd feel better after I dug his grave, even if I never got a chance to dump his body in it.

I meant to leave California, but I stopped in Soggy Lake, a wasteland far from civilization, the perfect place for me to lay low and dig. Three miles outside of the town, such that it was, I found a recess tucked between boulders, the surrounding soil broken, dry, and prone to crumbling, ideal for my needs.

I located a small apartment, paid for two months of rent in advance, and pretended I meant to lay down roots. My landlord didn't care what I did as long as he got paid.

I lazed during the day, and when I wasn't sleeping, I read books. Late at night, I dug. For two months, I battled the earth, winning inches of depth until I needed a rope to climb out of the hole. At the fifteen foot mark, nature smiled on me, as though it knew my heart and tried to appease some of my need for justice.

The soil grew dark, and the next night, I discovered water, amazed as it bubbled up, at first in a trickle, then strong enough to claim my shovel, my bucket, and my digging tools.

I laughed until I cried. I'd found water in the desert.

That was just my sort of luck.

Since digging hadn't accomplished anything, I abandoned my effort and went with what should have been my first plan: therapy.

If I could, I'd still drown the bastard and bury him, but until then, I needed to move on and find something *I* wanted to do with the rest of my life. Oil changes weren't it.

What was it, I had no idea, but a therapist might be able to help me figure it out. To go along with my plan of hiring a professional to pull me out of the mire I'd entrenched myself within, I'd live a dream I'd abandoned long ago.

I'd get a little cabin in the middle of nowhere, secluded, and as close to nature as I could go without leaving civilization altogether. Without my children, I didn't need to be anywhere or do anything.

I'd already messed up two attempts, which likely made 'mother' a job choice to avoid. Hestia had turned out perfectly, but her divinity played a role in that. I hadn't done her much justice; enduring me snapping couldn't have been easy for her, and divinity didn't grant her infallible sight. She couldn't teleport to places she'd never been. If she wanted to find me, she'd have to work for it, and I had no faith, not anymore.

Our broken family had served its purpose; it motivated her to do her job and work towards the preservation of the values needed for a house to become a home. Her magic was meant for one thing: to make families prosper.

My daughter was magnificent, and she'd only become a better woman—and goddess— over the years. Nolan would become a good man, unlike his father.

I could live with that.

My only regret was that I'd burned bridges with Viktor, using the lie of a smile to deter him. I still wasn't sure what he'd wanted out of our time together, but I missed his companionship.

Yep. I needed therapy. Adken had been my hell, and Viktor might've become my heaven, if only I'd given us a chance.

Sometimes, I truly was a fool.

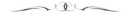

ON MY QUEST TO find a country home, I wandered to Colorado, where I discovered a cabin in the middle of nowhere for a little over twenty thousand dollars. The mountain had a tendency of burning every year, and the previous owner had tired of testing his luck, wanting to unload his five acres of land and the two-bedroom cabin with all the creature comforts I could want and a mix of solar panels and gas generator to power everything.

I loved everything about it, even the risk of it all going up in smoke. If I drove for an hour, I had a choice of two small towns, and if I sacrificed an extra twenty minutes, I could reach a young city, which boasted a large enough population to have therapists. To reach the city, I had to drive over twisting roads skirting precarious edges that dropped away to craggy valleys filled with tenacious pines.

I loved them, too.

To buy myself some privacy, I paid in cash and used my maiden name for the sale. The owner didn't care, and since he didn't want to be bothered with the bureaucracy, he signed over the deed and abandoned ship.

I spent a week turning the little cabin into a home, and once I was satisfied I'd made my mark on the mountain, I did what I'd come to Colorado to do. Hunting a therapist meant heading to the city, but instead of a doctor specialized in fixing broken people, I found Viktor.

Jumping around the corner made me a bad person, and I stole peeks at him.

He still checked off every last one of my boxes for the perfect man, and I adored him in his worn jeans.

On my third such peek, he arched a brow. "What are you doing?"

Busted. "Hiding so you don't spot me. Is it working?"

"You yelped before you ducked for cover. If you'd stayed quiet, maybe."

"Good to know." I stayed on my side of the corner and peeked again. "You're looking good."

He chuckled, leaned against the building, and made himself comfortable. Jeans suited him, and I contemplated kidnapping since my attempt at murder hadn't gone to plan. I could learn first-hand if he counted as therapy, and I had a brand-new bed.

"You have a twig in your hair."

I lifted my hand, and sure enough, there were pine needles stuck in my hair. "There's an attack pine near my house. It likes me."

Viktor closed the distance between us and picked pine needles out of my hair. "You're a difficult woman to find when you get it into your head to disappear, Dakota. Once I pried your maiden name out of your daughter, who is about ten minutes away from her first midlife crisis, I got a hit here, but I couldn't find the damned address I got a hit on. It's not on the bloody map!"

I laughed because I'd needed help from the previous owner to find it, too. "It's remote and private."

He sighed, plucked out a few more pine needles, and ran his fingers through my hair in a futile effort to untangle it. "I'm going to give you two choices. You can take me home with you, or you're coming home with me, but after spending two months looking for you, I'm not letting you out of my sight. Obviously, the fault's with me, as I should've given you strict instructions not to do anything crazy without me. Hestia's frantic from worry, and you have a court date in two weeks."

"I have a court date? Why? My appeal date isn't for another two months. I haven't done anything illegal."

Viktor arched a brow and waited.

"I haven't done anything illegal *yet*," I dutifully corrected.

Sighing, he took hold of my shoulders,

turned me away from the building, and marched me to the parking lot to an old dark gray SUV. "We figured the custody refusal had tripped your trigger. There's been a missing person bulletin out since you disappeared. It was a stupid mistake. The CDC didn't think to check the damned judge in charge of your case for beguilement. Adken had gotten to him, so he rejected your claim. A new judge has been reviewing the entire case, and you showing up in court is a formality. You'll be receiving the rest of your settlement and Nolan's custody. Nolan's already been informed, and his custody has been transferred temporarily."

I dug in my heels, twisting in Viktor's hold. "Who has custody?"

I flinched as my voice went up an octave.

"This is where things will get a bit weird," Viktor confessed, giving me a gentle push towards the SUV before releasing me and opening the passenger door. "I asked to be evaluated as a temporary guardian, and the CDC approved my claim after a nudge from Hestia. She approves of me."

My daughter might end up the death of me. "Because you don't snore and sleep in the nude."

Laughing, he leaned against his SUV and shook his head. "I tell her no. The instant the CDC realized I could get a fledgling divine to heel, they decided I could serve as a temporary guardian until you're settled. I'll confess, the first thing I did was have him transferred to a boarding school. There was a bit of resistance I wasn't expecting however."

"His tennis partner?" I suggested.

"I'm not going to ask how you knew that."

"Mother's intuition. He absolutely won't blame Latasha for their mutual losses, and he sent a few letters on the scraps of tennis practice schedules. When Adken's parents had custody, he stopped writing."

"The first thing I did was promise he'd be able to see you as soon as I found you. I explained things to him, and he understands why you're unbalanced right now. It'll get better, Dakota. I promise."

It wasn't fair. How could someone like Viktor, my living, breathing dream come true, pull miracles out of his ass and lay them at my feet?

"You got custody of my son."

He grimaced. "I didn't want him to go into the system, and Adken got his talent from his father. I didn't like the idea of Nolan being left with the family, and I demanded he be evaluated for beguilements. Seems like your resistance to beguilement's genetic, because Nolan's got a knack for it, too. It took a vampire, but he's been freed from his father's beguilements, too. As Adken's father has the same talent, I won the case. I challenged there was no way to verify a new beguilement couldn't be laid. Since my talent is used for rehabilitation, it was decided I was the best guardian in the meantime, as I could handle the consequences of long-term suppression. Fortunately, he wasn't difficult to handle. And no, he didn't need a succubus."

I climbed into the SUV, hesitated, and pointed at my junker. "That's my car."

"Would you be too angry with me if I had it towed to a junkyard for disposal? It looks like it's ready to fall apart."

I scowled. "It runs."

"I'm not sure how."

As I expected him to rightly give me the eye over my choice of vehicle, I decided to address the problem before it became a problem. "I didn't sell the Porsche. It's safely in storage, which is paid for six months. I was clearing my head until I could appeal for custody. I haven't *completely* snapped, thank you."

"Fair enough. What about the junker?"

"I probably should get rid of it," I confessed.

"I'll get rid of it so you don't have to worry about it."

"You need to stop being so nice. You're making this very difficult."

He smirked. "You want to take me home and indulge in my manliness, don't you?"

"If you keep insisting on being so nice, I might have to reevaluate my stance on men in my life, and that's not at all fair."

His smirk broadened to a grin. "How terrible. I do find it endlessly amusing I found you after becoming so frustrated I decided I needed a therapist. I figured if I needed a therapist, there was a chance you figured out you needed one, too."

"Guilty as charged. I'm definitely in need of therapy, although you'll do for tonight."

"Just for tonight?"

I liked the idea enough I met his grin with one of my own. "We'll play it by ear."

He chuckled, closed the passenger door, and circled his SUV, sliding behind the wheel. He fit appropriately, and I nodded my approval while buckling my seatbelt.

When he started the engine without a word, I added, "I dug a hole and found a spring, but I didn't have anyone to toss in, so I came here."

"You really should give Hestia a call."

I shook my head. "She doesn't need me and my instability ruining her plans. Right now, I'll get in her way. She was busy."

Viktor shot a glare at me. "I told her she needed to be more careful. Dakota, she's young and discovering the world. You've taught her a very important lesson about taking people for granted. She needs to know her mother is all right just as much as you need some TLC from her. Now, that said, I should take you home. That I couldn't find it is driving me absolutely insane."

"It's a long drive down narrow, twisting roads. We could go to a hotel instead."

"I'd like to see your house. It'll give me a good idea of the type of home you like."

"It's a tiny cabin in the middle of the woods."

"Not what I was expecting, but I can roll with that. Where am I going?"

I gave him directions to my cabin. Once on the road, he glanced at me out of the corner of his eye. "I have some news for you, but I'm not sure if it's good news or bad news."

"Tell me."

"I know where the bastard is, and I know exactly how we can get our hands on him, but you'll need to be the bait. If we do this just right, we can commit the perfect murder. It'll be legal in the eyes of the law, written off as self-defense without punishment and barred from our records."

I had to be dreaming, so I pinched myself to check. I yelped at the flash of pain, staring at the crescent mark on the back of my hand. "You really think we can get away with murder?"

"We tell him where you are, and if he

comes for you as I expect he will, it's self-defense. That we'd be ready for him doesn't change the verdict. The CDC has already issued a bulletin for him authorizing lethal force. If he uses his magic on you or touches you, I can kill him without penalty. We just have to lure him out, which will be very simple."

"I'd like to help kill him," I complained.

"The reality is, he'll blank slate you, so the killing will fall to me. You'll have to trust me, because if I fuck this up, you'll be in his hands. It's risky."

"He used his magic on Nolan," I snarled.

"I know, I know. Nolan's safe from him, as is Hestia. Hestia knows what he looks like, and I've told her I'll light her ass on fire if she doesn't teleport away the instant she spots him. He'd have to catch her completely off guard, and I don't see that happening right now. She's jumpy."

"Jumpy?"

"Once she knows I've found you, I'm sure she'll drive us both insane with her matchmaking efforts. She's determined, I'll give her that."

"I'm so sorry."

"Don't be. It's not every day a goddess rather explicitly tells me what I should be doing with her mother. I haven't laughed so hard in years. She wasn't happy I started laughing, but I couldn't help it. She has no idea I've enjoyed every minute spent exploring you. I'm hoping you'll invite me into your home and allow me to repeat the experience."

"It'd be cruel to leave you to the tender mercies of the attack pine."

"I think I owe you some murderous pillow talk, too."

"I dug a nice hole in California. Weren't you the one who told me to dig it so deep no one would find the bastard? We could still go with our first plan."

"We could, but I have a condition." He smirked, turning his attention to the road.

"What?"

"When we're done, you'll owe me a favor, which I'll ask over his dead body."

What sort of favor could Viktor want from me? Whatever it was, it'd be worth it. "You have a deal."

EIGHT

We're going to need a new hole.

ADKEN WAS HIDING near Reno where the city and the Sierra Nevada clashed, far enough from civilization no one would hear him scream. Cabins just like the one Adken owned were available for rent, and after a dozen calls, I was able to reserve one within three miles of where my ex-husband hid.

"We're going to need a new hole," I complained to my partner in crime, looking over the map marking where my ex lurked. "Mine's too far away."

Viktor stretched out beside me in bed, hard at work twirling my hair around a finger. "We can't afford to wait two months for you to dig a new hole. I'm sorry."

"It'll be a lot faster if you're helping me dig. Two people can dig a grave overnight. I bet can manage in three nights flat. I took my time digging my hole. You seduced me with that plan, Viktor. It seems like a waste not to use such a pleasant memory."

He chuckled and continued playing with my hair. "You have a delightfully vicious side to you, Dakota."

"You like it. I want to dig a hole and bury the bastard."

"And what about your hope to drown him?"

"I'm willing to make some concessions, but damn it, I want that hole."

"The hole's going to cost you one additional favor over his dead body."

"It better be a damned good hole," I muttered.

Viktor laughed so hard he cried. "It'll be the best hole I can give you. When's the reservation for?"

"The cabin's vacant, so we can go over as soon as tomorrow. I took it for two weeks. I'm not going to miss my court date, am I? It'd look bad if I didn't make my court date because I was too busy killing Adken. If we're killing him legally, we don't really need a hole, do we?"

"No, we don't, but I'll help you dig one anyway. It'll be therapeutic. It'll take a few days to get set up and lure him to us. He's mostly hiding in his cabin, so we're going to have to drop a few hints with one of his minions. He has a few in Reno doing errands for him. They're beguiled, but it's basic compared to what he did to you. The CDC will take care of them once he's out of the way."

"I can live with that. It can be a celebratory hole, completely symbolic. I'd be nice if he just disappeared, but…" I shrugged. "Him being gone is enough for me."

"Yet you're paying me in a favor to help you dig a hole."

"You seemed so hopeful. I couldn't deny you a chance for a second favor, especially not when you lived up to your promise of murderous pillow talk."

"I aim to please."

That he did.

WE DROVE to Reno the following morning, and to reach the cabin I'd rented, we had to drive past where Adken hid. I would've been content to pass the place, but a flash of gold drew my eye, and I slapped my hand to the passenger window. "Stop the car," I barked.

Viktor obeyed, not quite slamming the brakes, but hard enough the SUV skidded on the loose gravel. "What the…?"

I held up my hand, pressed my nose to the glass, and stared at the source of the color, the same shade as my hair.

Yep, I recognized the pretty little blonde

head hiding in the bushes, and I seriously contemplated Viktor's advice to leash my daughter. Worse, there was a second head of darker hair beside her, skirting the line between a golden chestnut and a mousy brown, which put the figure at a high risk of being my first-born child.

"Viktor?" I growled, contemplating how much at fault the man beside me was for the escapees loitering near Adken's hideout.

"I know that sound. That's the sound of an angry woman who's about to murder me. What did I do?"

"I think there were some escapees."

"Escapees…?" Viktor leaned towards me, and when I pointed at the pair hiding in the bushes, he cursed. He cursed so much I raised my eyebrows at the expletives pouring out of his mouth.

"Viktor…"

"I had nothing to do with this. I'd never encourage that havoc-wreaking hellion to join in a murder."

Oops. "I'll take the blame for that. I told her I wanted to kill the bastard and might need her help hiding the body."

The look Viktor shot me should've struck me dead. "We're going to have a long talk over giving impressionable goddesses bad ideas."

"First, we stop those monsters from doing

something I regret," I hissed, unbuckling my seatbelt. "Then, you're going to explain how they found their way here."

"Well, Nolan was the one who told us all of his father's properties. This was one of them. That's my fault. I did tell him I'd make sure his father was out of the way."

"You no longer have any grounds to chastise me for giving impressionable children bad ideas."

He blinked, and he furrowed his brows. "Huh. I guess you're right. I'm never going to win a parenting award, am I?"

"Don't worry. Neither will I. I'm playing with a handicap, though. I have a goddess to contend with. I'm pretty sure she counts as a parenting nightmare."

"I left the older brat at boarding school, I swear," Viktor muttered.

"I produce brats, don't I?" I slumped in my seat. "This is all my fault."

Viktor ground his knuckles against the top of my head. "You take the girl, I'll grab the boy, and try not to stampede through the bushes like an elephant. I recommend slapping your hand over her mouth to stop the screams."

"Screaming would definitely alert Adken."

"Yes, it would." Viktor sighed, unbuckled his belt, and eased open his door. "Be very, very quiet. We're hunting children."

I clamped my lips together so I wouldn't giggle. "You're a bad, bad man, Viktor."

"But you like it," he whispered, slipping out of his SUV. To limit the noise, he left his door open, and I followed his example.

Fortunately for both of us, my children were so absorbed in their spying they didn't notice us creep up behind them. At Viktor's silent signal, I clapped my hand over my daughter's mouth while Viktor jumped my son, who had at least several inches on me.

Hestia gasped.

"Shh," I hissed. While my daughter was stiff in my hold, she didn't fight me when I pulled her away from the bushes in the direction of Viktor's SUV. "What do you think you're doing, young lady?" I demanded in a whisper.

"Mom?" my daughter squeaked.

I hauled my demonic divine entity of a child to the SUV, an arm wrapped around her throat so she wouldn't escape. "I've been called that from time to time. You have a lot of explaining to do, missy! Just what do you think you're doing here?"

"I was rescuing you!" she replied, her voice dipping into a whine.

"You were *what*?" I took a deep breath so I wouldn't turn my daughter over my knee and spank her for putting herself in danger. "I was never in need of rescue, but the sentiment is appreciated. I'm pretty sure you were told to avoid him at all costs, Hestia. This is not avoiding him. This is deliberately putting yourself in harm's way."

Capturing my daughter in a headlock, I dragged her the rest of the way to the SUV, opened the back door, and shoved her in. She scrambled inside, her eyes wide and mouth hanging open. When she froze, I snapped my fingers and pointed at the seatbelt. Her hands shook, but she obeyed.

Viktor had an easier time with Nolan, who took the hint, scrambled around the vehicle, and climbed in beside his half-sister, fumbling with the belt before he could earn himself a scolding.

Nolan was taller than me, and in a fortuitous roll of the genetic dice, he took after me more than he did his father. I looked over both my children, who watched me with owl-wide eyes, and reclaimed the front seat while Viktor hopped behind the wheel.

"I'm gonna tan your hides," Viktor announced before starting the engine. "What the hell were you thinking?"

I grinned.

"We thought he'd gotten hold of Mom!" my daughter wailed. "He hadn't?"

"Obviously not," I muttered, shaking my head. "No. I was enjoying an unconventional vacation. Viktor decided to come along for the ride. It was the adult version of hide and go seek. Viktor's really bad at the game. If you play and he's the seeker, he might leave you waiting for a few months."

Viktor sighed and drove us to the cabin I'd rented. "I'm in trouble because I assured your mother you were safe and sound in boarding school. Which is where you should have been, Nolan. Care to explain why you aren't where I left you a few days ago?"

"Hestia busted me out to show her how to get here."

Of course she did. My daughter viewed rules as things to be broken with limited exceptions. "Hestia! I've a mind to leash you."

"Mom," my daughter whined. "It's not my fault! I thought the sperm donor had grabbed you."

"I've a mind to actually let Viktor tan your ass, young lady. While I have opinions about him, he *is* Nolan's father."

"I call him the asshole," my son said, and I glanced in the rearview mirror in time to watch my son shrug.

"Nolan has opinions similar to his sister's," Viktor murmured. "You two kids hush back there. Your mother and I are in the middle of committing a murder, and we weren't expecting a pair of tagalongs. I'm the manual labor, and if you're not careful, you're going to be recruited to help. I've been tasked with digging her a hole. Ironically, we won't be using this hole to hide the body, as we're going to lure the asshole over to our cabin nearby. When he gets within ten feet of her of his own volition, it's a legal kill."

"Way to teach them good morals," I muttered.

"There's no point in hiding it, and since we're luring the bastard to our cabin, it's a good idea to warn them there's going to be bloodshed."

I scowled. "Where can I get leashes appropriate for children?"

The children in question chorused, "Mom!"

That my son knew me at all after so many years made me want to cry.

"Pipe down, kids. I really will tan your hides if you make your mother cry. I already ruined her plans to hide the body, so let's not stir her ire any more. She might send us all to bed without supper if we're not good."

"I'd never," I protested. "Well, maybe you. I'd never starve my children, no matter how much they might deserve it for going near a dangerous person."

The whined apologies from the backseat made me grin.

"This does change our plan," Viktor said, turning onto the path that'd lead to our cabin. "Two kids were not part of the picture."

"They can stick with you, and I'll do my part just as planned. When he shows up and knocks, I'll answer, you take care of the rest." I shrugged. "Just as long as the demonic entities in the back promise they'll do exactly as told."

"Kids, the original plan was for your mother to be the bait and lure him out. We're expecting him to use his magic, which is what will allow me to use the kill authority granted by the CDC. For a while, she might not be herself. If I can undo it, I will, but I expect I'll have to call in a vampire. If he acts true to form, he'll blank slate her. Here's the important part of this, kids. Just because we're ready for him does *not* mean we're actually planning his death. We're just being really prepared if he tries another stunt like the one in Vegas."

"Can I help?" Nolan asked. "The asshole used his magic on me, too."

"No." Viktor parked, twisted around so he could look into the back, and pointed at my son. "Under no circumstances will you help. Your mother will blame me if anything happens to you, and I'm really hoping she's planning on keeping me around, so don't you ruin my chances, you runty brat."

I turned in time to see my son grin like a little idiot at Viktor.

Men.

"He's hardly runty," I protested.

"You're biased," Viktor countered, winking at me. "While I'm a fan of awkward and teary reunions, I'd be grateful if that could wait until *after* the ex is dealt with. Permanently."

"He has an ulterior motive, Mom. It involves getting rid of the old competition so he can have you all to himself," my daughter announced. "My brother and I have already discussed it, and we're giving him our permission to court you."

"To court me?" I blurted.

My children were going to be so disappointed if they ever found out I had severe problems with keeping my hands off Viktor on a good day.

"You deserve better than what the asshole did to you," my son confessed.

Would I ever be able to truly move on from the heartache of the past? I'd have to for the sake of my son, who I didn't even know. My chance to learn everything about him had finally come, as long as I didn't mess everything up. "Nolan, what he did was never your fault. It wasn't mine, either."

Viktor smiled at me, and the tenderness in his expression both broke my heart and healed it all at the same time. That Nolan's expression matched wrecked me and put me back together again.

The only future I needed was in the SUV with me.

"I'm a practical woman. Courting sounds like too much work."

Viktor snickered, and with the faintest of leers, he got out of his SUV. "I wonder why."

"You'll pay for that later," I promised.

"I look forward to it."

Rolling my eyes, I got out of the vehicle, went to the back, and opened the back door, staring down at my son with my throat tight as though my heart had tried to escape and hadn't quite made it. Swallowing, I tried not to think of everything I'd missed over the years.

He unbuckled his seat belt, leaned towards me, and kissed my cheek. "You're exactly like I remember."

My eyes burned, and I reached for him, cupping his face in my hands. Not only was he taller than me, I wouldn't have recognized him in a crowd. I wouldn't have recognized him at all.

My heart hurt, and I wasn't sure the pain would ever go away.

"You've grown so much." The words were the only ones I could say without lying.

Viktor came to my rescue, grabbed me by the waist, pulled me back, and tossed me over his shoulder. I squealed, clutching the back of his shirt, eyes wide as I comprehended he'd picked me up with no effort. "One of you will cry, then both of you will cry, and then Hestia and I will be trying to get you both to stop crying, but she'll start crying, too. I'll go mad. After the menace has been dealt with, you can indulge. You'll have to put yourselves back together before your mother's court date, however, so I'm pulling the plug on any breakdowns then."

I peered around Viktor. Nolan saluted while Hestia giggled.

"Now that we have an understanding, I'm going to take your mother inside and give her a few minutes to regain her composure. While I'm gone, you two stay here. You can discuss things you can do to help from a safe distance, all right? And Hestia, I meant it. If he looks like he's going to touch you, you teleport away. Your mother will never forgive herself if something happens to you because of him. Understood?"

My daughter hung her head and mumbled something.

Viktor cleared his throat.

"Yes, sir," she whispered.

VIKTOR CHEATED, and I learned a very important lesson about his talent and the nature of consent. A claim I trusted him fulfilled the condition of his talent, and the instant I'd answered yes to his innocent-seeming question, the bastard made me take an unexpected nap, effectively knocking me out of action for the rest of the day and the night.

I should've resented him, but I enjoyed waking up with him stretched out beside me, his arm pinning me against his chest. He didn't snore, but I enjoyed listening to his slow, steady breaths. As he had since our first time together, he slept in the nude, which made me hope neither of my children waltzed in as children did whenever they wanted something.

"You rat," I hissed.

A soft chuckle and his breath against the back of my neck promised he wasn't asleep. "You were tired, you needed the rest, and I'm not sorry. Good morning. With some help from the children, I've dug you a beautiful hole half a mile from here. It's more of a rock shaft, as it seems Nolan's a talented elementalist. Tunneling through stone isn't a challenge for him, although he wasn't expecting to hit a spring on his way down. We got thoroughly soaked. He carved a channel so the cabin wouldn't flood, but I'm afraid the area's going to have a new stream unless it dries out fast."

"Huh. I found a spring, too."

"Did you use magic to dig your hole?"

"No. I used a shovel."

"You will owe me that second favor over your ex's dead body."

While I'd expected him to use a shovel, I couldn't blame him for taking advantage of magic. Given a choice, I would've done the same. Digging a hole was hard work, and there was no way I'd be able to dig a hole through solid rock. "I only demanded a hole," I conceded.

"I'm a terrible cheater, and I used the same trick on the kids I used on you. They'll be down until noon at the earliest, giving us plenty of time to do anything nefarious you may have in mind."

"What sort of nefarious? I can think of several nefarious things we could do," I admitted.

"Whatever you want."

I reached for the nightstand and grabbed his cell to check the time. I had three hours to implement any nefarious plans. "Is three hours really long enough? I'm not sure we can do all that *and* murder my ex in three hours, Viktor."

"Nolan's going to be our mole. He's still talking with his grandparents, and he's going to tell them I'm arranging for him to meet you here in Reno, as you enjoy the outdoors and it's on neutral turf. News should get to your ex by tonight, as I'm positive the bastard is still in contact with his parents about Nolan. I have a theory."

"Which is?"

"Nolan isn't pliable enough; he's too much of his mother's son, which isn't what your ex needs in an heir, so he's gunning for another heir. Why he isn't just remarrying, I don't know."

"I divorced him, not the other way around. He probably feels he's entitled to me despite the divorce." I knew so; he'd told me as much himself when I was leaving the courthouse, determined never to see him again if I had anything to do with it.

That hadn't worked out well for me.

"Not on my watch," Viktor hissed through clenched teeth.

"Well, you *are* going to help me kill him. I'm pretty sure this makes us bad people. Terrible villains, even. They should send people like us to jail."

Viktor snorted. "If he's going to treat you like a broodmare, I'm going to put him down like the rabid animal he is. Men like him don't reform. Once a predator, always a predator. He was willing to circumvent your free will to get what he wanted. Given the chance, he'll do it to someone else, someone who doesn't have your natural resilience. Worse, I could've been just like him, too."

"But you're not."

"I cheated and put you to sleep," he reminded me. "I couldn't handle any of you crying."

"It's going to happen."

"It wasn't happening yesterday. I was originally going to make Nolan dig with a shovel until he looked at me like I was insane and asked why he couldn't use magic. A hole, according to him, is a hole."

"I'm relieved he's got some grasp of practicality and common sense."

"I'd withhold judgment on the common sense part," Viktor warned. "He did join forces with Hestia, and they were planning to assault your ex. They were armed with a pocket knife."

I groaned. "What are you going to be armed with, anyway?"

"A gun."

"And you actually know how to use it?"

"I've been trained, but I'm planning on getting up close and personal with him. Hard to miss at point blank range. I'm not taking any chances with the bastard. I'm going to come up behind him when he's focused on you. It's going to be messy. Nolan wanted to electrocute him, but I said no. Using yourself as bait is one thing, but I thought you'd lose your shit if Nolan was involved. Honestly, I let Nolan dig the hole because he wanted to help. You should be thanking me for stopping that train wreck."

"I am."

"I'd like it a lot if you showed me how grateful you are."

I bet he would, and as I'd enjoy it, too, I did.

NINE

Justice came in many flavors.

EVERY MURDER HAD SEVERAL COMPONENTS, and any detective worth his badge would know who was behind my ex-husband's impending demise.

Motive was easy. I wanted Adken dead for ruining my life, Viktor wanted to get rid of the competition, and I tried not to think too hard of my son's motivations. A young man shouldn't have been burdened with the thoughts of killing his father, even though those reasons were good ones.

A detective would have some sympathy for my son, but it wouldn't spare us from our crimes.

Therapy wouldn't erase the sort of violations we'd both suffered, although Adken's death would close the book on that miserable part of our lives and give us a chance to move on without fear. Prison wouldn't work on a man like Adken, not on a man who could sway his guards with touch or word. According to Viktor, not even solitary confinement could keep a puppeteer detained long.

Their touch became law, and it took only a single mistake for prison to lose its effectiveness.

After motive came the method, and while there had been more elaborate plans than ours, ours stood a good chance of working—and was easy to decipher. There wasn't hiding a bullet to the brain, and it wouldn't take long for a smart detective to piece together we'd lured Adken to his death.

Adken developed tunnel vision when he found something he wanted, and we were counting on that to blind him to Viktor's ambush.

At first, I'd considered arming myself with a knife, but Viktor didn't want to give Adken any weapons.

Defying my lover had taken every scrap of my will, but I'd picked up a chunk of razor stone, clutching it and challenging him with a glare. While he watched, I'd stuffed my rock in my pocket.

He made no mention of the stone, and I ignored the scrapes on my fingers and the new hole in my jeans.

After method came the murder and the madness, which involved hiding just enough evidence of our wrongdoing to clear us in the courts, which would use an angel to verify the truth. Everything we said, everything we thought, and everything we did would face scrutiny.

Viktor thought we could get away with it, as long as we stuck to the truth. Our version of the truth amused me, boiling down to me needing to escape life while Viktor wanted to become a part of my life. He wanted to present it as a chance to see if we could share living space without getting sick of each other.

Assuming neither of my children were in the session, I'd cheerfully admit I just wanted to get him out of his pants.

Adken showing up would be something we feared and expected, which was true. An angel might notice the subtle differences, but angels had a sense of justice, one that went beyond the letter of the law.

Justice came in many flavors, and angels obeyed the spirit of the law. The spirit was so often not the letter, so Viktor believed they'd side with us. From my understanding of the situation, Viktor would be trying our case in a way the courts didn't intend, convincing the angel to side with us through his thoughts.

On the surface, law enforcement seemed murky, but everything Viktor implied made it a far scarier thing.

From the day I'd been born, I'd been

taught angels were the purest form of the truth, unable to be swayed by anyone. Viktor's knowing smile and shrug undermined everything I'd believed.

I wondered what life after the murder would be like. Would the weight of taking someone else's life change me?

Likely, but I needed the closure Adken's death would provide. If our case stood up in the courts, the verdict would offer the illusion of legitimacy.

I could live with illusions if it meant I could breathe without the worry of him coming for me or my children ever again.

As though understanding I needed time to come to terms with what we planned to do, Viktor coached Nolan on what to tell his grandparents to make them unwitting accessories in Adken's demise.

It didn't take me long. The thought of dancing on his grave, possibly naked if circumstances allowed, did a good job of confirming I really wanted to rid the world of the bastard. Later, guilt would gnaw at me for involving Viktor in my problems, and no matter what favors he asked of me, it'd never be enough to repay him for his help.

A lifetime in prison was worth irrevocable freedom from Adken and his magic.

As soon as Nolan called his grandparents, the clock would begin ticking. If they did as

Viktor believed, we could have an unwanted visitor within minutes. My job was simple.

All I had to do was open the door when he arrived. In reality, I wouldn't last long. Adken would use his magic on me as quickly as he could, trapping me within my body. I'd be aware of nothing once he touched me.

The stone in my pocket was nothing more than a symbol, proof I could—and would—stand up for myself with Viktor. Adken wouldn't view a rock as a weapon.

He'd find my symbol worthless.

I trusted Viktor to protect my children, and they waited outside with him. The only person to be trapped in the cabin would be me, no matter what Adken did.

The knock came far sooner than I expected, and with shaking heads, I obeyed our plan, feigning ignorance my ex-husband would show. I opened the door, and the instant I recognized Adken, I sucked in a breath, forcing my eyes wide. "You."

"Dakota. You're really here. Good."

I tightened my grip on my shard, and the edges sliced into my fingers. "What do you want?"

He dismissed my question with a wave of his hand, stepping closer. "It doesn't matter. You're not going to be capable of caring soon enough. I gave you a chance to come peacefully. Now I'm just going to take what I want, and you're going to produce a worthwhile heir for me this time."

We moved at the same time. He touched my cheek, I yanked my shard out of my pocket, lifted my arm, and struck for the only place I thought my rock might do some damage, the soft skin of his throat.

As it had in Vegas, Adken's magic numbed my skin, made me tingle, and smothered me in darkness, sucking me into a void disconnected from everything, even my body.

I didn't even know if I'd hit him with my defiant blow.

Unable to do anything else, I dreamed of his blood on my hand, his body twitching as he breathed his last. I dreamed of the moment he sighed, the life fleeing from his body.

All my hopes rode with Viktor and his gun, freeing me and my children from our living nightmare.

A sharp slap across the face jerked me out of the abyss, and light assaulted my eyes. I yelped, turning my head to escape, but a softer touch to my cheek held me still.

"Dakota?" Viktor demanded, and he leaned close, touching his brow to mine. "Are you all right?"

"Damn it. The bastard got me," I complained, my tongue refusing to cooperate without slurring.

"You're something else. The fucker blank

slated you, and you still went for his jugular with your damned rock!" Viktor shook my shoulders. "You scared the liver out of me. Tearing his jugular open was *not* part of our plan. Are you trying to give me a heart attack? If so, you almost succeeded. *I thought he had killed you!*"

I gaped at him. "What?"

Viktor's grip on my shoulders tightened. "When the jugular's severed, it can cause a rather dramatic fountaining of blood. He reached for you, blood sprayed, and you both went down in a heap. When I reached you, you were covered in blood. You scared the kids." Sighing, he relaxed his hold, sliding his arms down my arms, which were covered in blood. "I've a mind to turn you over my knee for scaring us so much. I sent the kids to the SUV, and Hestia's calling the police. It's an open and close self-defense case."

"Oh." I lowered my gaze to my shirt, which was rather wet and stained with dark splotches. "Ew. I'm wearing my ex."

Viktor laughed and ground his knuckles against the top of my head. "You little idiot."

Laughing, I nodded. "I'm an idiot. I'm an idiot who owes you two favors over his dead body."

I had no idea where his dead body was, but I didn't want to see it, so I admired Viktor instead, who had blood splotched on his face, hands, and shirt, too.

"I'm impressed. He hit you so hard I felt the magic all the way where I was hiding. I can't even claim the kill. I may have added a bullet or two to make sure he stayed down, but you did the real work." His smile devastated me. "For favor one, you must come live with me and share my bed each and every night until we're both old and wrinkled. Once you're able to stand without help, I'll get on my knees and beg until you agree to be my wife. I'll do it every day in an increasingly more embarrassing way until you agree."

I sucked in a breath, my eyes widening. "That's one hell of a favor, Viktor."

"That was the deal, Future Mrs. Jenkins. You agreed to *anything* I wanted, and I want you. If I have to beg every day for the rest of our lives, so be it."

"Begging won't be necessary." He amazed me; I couldn't imagine why he'd want me as much as I wanted him, but I wasn't going to throw away a chance for the sort of family and home Adken had never been able to offer me. "And your second favor?"

"Favor number two is even more important me to the first one, and that one means the world to me."

Uh oh. "Does it involve having more children?"

More children appealed to me, especially knowing they'd have a father who'd love them.

"Not quite."

I frowned, unable to think of what else he could possibly want more important than convincing me to spend the rest of my life with him. "What's the favor?"

"I need you to forgive me."

"What? For what? You've done nothing wrong."

"Oh, I've done a lot wrong, but I'll start with my gravest sin."

I waited, at a loss of what he could've done that he'd confess it over my ex's dead body.

"Several years ago, I met an ice queen in a bar so drunk—"

Realization slammed into me and I grabbed handfuls of my hair, giving a headache-inducing yank. "You have got to be kidding me!"

Viktor gulped. "Hestia was vetting me because she wanted to know about her father, so she decided to ask the CDC to identify me before she matures as a goddess, which might erase paternal and maternal DNA evidence. As I'm a CDC employee, my DNA sample was in the system. The reason she was skipping on Sundays was so she could meet with me, but she was afraid to tell you, as she didn't know how you'd react. She'd seen how you reacted when your child support statements came in, so she didn't want to upset you."

My mouth dropped open, but I couldn't force out a single word. Viktor waited.

And waited. And waited.

"T-that conniving little brat was trying to set me up with her own father!"

Viktor's face darkened in a blush. "That's accurate."

"You're really the poor man I violated in a bar?"

"It wasn't in a bar. I took you home with me, and I assure you, I was a most willing participant. I wanted to tell you sooner, but you were so determined to be the perfect mother, and you didn't want to burden anyone, that I couldn't force myself to do it. I figured I'd bide my time and see what happened. Then Adken blank slated you. The CDC knew Hestia was our daughter, so they approved my request to be the one to stay with you after the suppressors were removed." He lifted his hand and ran his fingers through his hair. "You're not a burden, and neither is she, and if you agree to forgive me, I swear I'll do my best to keep from disappointing you. Whatever you want, I'll give it to you."

Was he kidding? It'd take work to adjust, adapt, and accept reality, but he was giving me the final choice.

He would beg, but he wouldn't force.

"You've already given me everything I could want."

"What? How?"

I allowed myself a grim smile. "You dug me a hole, just like I wanted, although it doesn't look like we need it—and Nolan did most of the work. On my own, I'd only have a badly dug hole and no body to put in it. Without you, I'd still be trapped in his shadow."

"I should've followed you home years ago."

"Like a sexy stalker puppy?" I rolled my eyes. "Please. I'm an independent woman in need of therapy here."

"I like how you admit you need therapy."

"I killed my ex with a sharp rock, and I'm seriously contemplating dumping his body in a hole my lover dug with a lot of help from my son. I'm pretty sure we all need therapy."

"We'll figure something out," he promised. "If you really need therapy, I'll go with you to every session."

"Do you think we can get away with dumping his body?"

"I'm afraid not. It'd be too much work. Why mess with your easy self-defense verdict? And to think people say there's no such thing as the perfect murder. Well done, Future Mrs. Jenkins."

I couldn't help it; I laughed. "Hey, Viktor?"

"What?"

"Do I lose my independent woman status if you have to carry me to the SUV? I don't think my legs are ready to work quite right, and for some reason, I don't think I want to stay here tonight," I confessed.

"No, but only if you agree to both of my favors. I'll even carry you like the pretty princess you are rather than toss you over my shoulder while grunting like a caveman."

"Deal. I'd say we should seal the deal with a kiss, but I'm covered in blood for some reason."

He kissed me anyway. "What's a little blood between friends?"

SERIAL KILLER PRINCESS is the next book in the Magical Romantic Comedy (with a body count) series. These stories, with the exception of Burn, Baby, Burn (sequel to Playing with Fire,) can be read in any order.

About R.J. Blain

Want to hear from the author when a new book releases? You can sign up at her website (thesneakykittycritic.com). Please note this newsletter is operated by the Furred & Frond Management. Expect to be sassed by a cat. (With guest features of other animals, including dogs.)

A complete list of books written by RJ and her various pen names is available at https://books2read.com/rl/The-Fantasy-Worlds-of-RJ-Blain.

RJ BLAIN suffers from a Moleskine journal obsession, a pen fixation, and a terrible tendency to pun without warning.

When she isn't playing pretend, she likes to think she's a cartographer and a sumi-e painter.

In her spare time, she daydreams about being a spy. Should that fail, her contingency plan involves tying her best of enemies to spinning wheels and quoting James Bond villains until she is satisfied.

RJ also writes as Susan Copperfield and Bernadette Franklin. Visit RJ and her pets (the Management) at thesneakykittycritic.com.

FOLLOW RJ & HER ALTER EGOS ON BOOKBUB:
RJ BLAIN
SUSAN COPPERFIELD
BERNADETTE FRANKLIN